Readers love
Connie Bailey

Miles to Go

"I loved this book from start to finish and couldn't put it down."
—Rainbow Reviews

Kaji Sukoshi and The Shining One

"… subtle, touching, sweet and understated."
—Fallen Angels Reviews

True Blue

"An excellent book not to be missed."
—Literary Nymphs

REVENANT

CONNIE BAILEY

Dreamspinner Press

Published by
Dreamspinner Press
4760 Preston Road
Suite 244-149
Frisco, TX 75034
http://www.dreamspinnerpress.com/

Revenant

Cover Art by Christine Griffin, alizarin_griffin@yahoo.com
http://christinegriffin.artworkfolio.com/
Cover Design by Mara McKennen

ISBN: 978-1-61581-454-1

Printed in the United States of America
Second Edition
April, 2010

eBook edition available
eBook ISBN: 978-1-61581-402-2

To the staff of Dreamspinner, the press with a heart.

Prologue

CILLIAN stepped out of the small rowboat into the cold nighttime waters around the islet of Ynys Gwarchodwr. Pulling the light craft up onto the rocky shore, the young Welshman staggered up the steep incline, cursing under his breath. At least it wasn't far to Castle Guard; the medieval pile of stone took up most of the small island it crouched on. Across the sound, the young man could see the paltry lights of the village of Drws Cefnforoedd on the mainland. Deliberately, Cillian hawked phlegm and spat in the direction of the home he couldn't wait to leave. This clandestine meeting with his lover was the most exciting thing that had happened to him in his eighteen years on Earth, and he went eagerly through the dark fortress gate.

He moved swiftly across the bailey and into the main building until his foot caught on a piece of loose masonry in the great hall and he went sprawling. Calling on the saints to witness the malicious intent of the obstacle that had tripped him, Cillian made sure that the bottle Morgan had procured for him wasn't broken. He rose to his knees, dug a disposable lighter from the pocket of his worn jeans, and flicked it. The tiny flame and the scant moonlight that found its way through gaps in the ceiling did little to dispel the oppressive gloom of nine centuries and thousands of tons of ancient stone. Opening the bottle, Cillian tried drowning his nervousness over the trysting place in a few inches of whiskey, but his anxiety refused to die—for a few good reasons.

Chief among them was the indisputable fact that Cillian was trespassing. The island and fortress of Caer Gwarchod belonged to Lord Turcotte, and though the peer lived in London, Cillian knew the man wouldn't take kindly to prowlers on his property, whatever their purpose. Cillian didn't know the lord personally—not the likes of him—but Turcotte's reputation for being a hard and unforgiving man was well-known in the village. If Cillian were caught here, he didn't think that even his lover's high position in the community would afford him any mercy.

"Sod Lord Turcotte and all his ancestors," Cillian shouted with drunken bravado as the lighter grew too hot to hold. "Sod the whole lot of bleedin' toffee-nosed gits thinkin' they're better than me."

Giggling at his daring, the young man took another drink. Cillian's lover, Sean, didn't like it when he drank, but damned if he would wait in this haunted place without a drop of something to stiffen his spine. He didn't believe in ghosts as a general rule, but here in the old castle after dark, it was hard not to imagine bloodthirsty ghoulies and goblins in every corner. Cillian took another pull at the bottle and willed his man to hurry. Thinking of Sean and what they'd be doing in a little while made Cillian's half-a-hard-on pulse eagerly.

Setting the whiskey aside, he slipped a hand down his flat belly and under his waistband. Eyes half-closed, he fondled himself idly, lulled by the rhythmic crash of the surf against the rocks. He was starting to get serious about having a wank when an odd noise stopped him in mid-stroke. The high-pitched ringing sound, like a fingertip rubbed lightly along the rim of a crystal wine glass, came from the direction of the sweeping double staircase, but Cillian could see nothing in the welter of deep shadows.

It occurred to the young man that his lover might have arrived before him and was watching him toss off. "Sean?" he called softly. "Is that you, love?"

Behind Cillian, the grainy moonlight began to thicken. Minute motes of argent radiance charged by some arcane force flew together like iron filings in a magnetic field, forming a column of shimmering silver. Cillian felt a sudden chill on the back of his neck and turned to look behind him. Leaping to his feet, he stared, wide-eyed, as the swarming sparks of light coalesced into the shape of a man. The ghost—for what else could it be—fixed its pale gaze on the young man. The strong, aquiline features of the softly glowing face looked tantalizingly familiar to Cillian, but he was too stunned to try to identify the phantom. His astonishment quickly metastasized to rank fear as the spectral stranger reached out a hand to curse him... or worse. The nameless dread of being touched by the thing was instantaneous and overwhelming.

"G-get away from me!" Cillian stammered as he spun away from the ghost and started to run.

The apparition swooped forward, snaking its arm around the young man's neck before Cillian had taken two steps. Cillian was yanked back and then up, his feet dangling several inches above the ground as his breath was choked off. He struggled, but his flailing limbs met nothing but air. Only the arm that held him aloft and the cold lips pressed to his throat seemed to have any substance, but he felt the ghost behind him gain solidity with each passing moment until he was held fast against a broad chest by two muscular arms. Cillian ceased thrashing and went limp as he struggled to drag breath into his burning lungs. Instantly, the pressure on his windpipe eased, and he was lowered until he could stand. As he was turned to face his captor, Cillian closed his eyes, shivering from terror and the wintry chill that the spirit exuded.

"Whuh-what do yuh-you wuh-wuh-want?" he said through chattering teeth.

The ghost made no answer, reveling in the rising spiral of its victim's horror, relishing the mortal's blind fear of an unknown fate. Yes, the fear was good, sharp and intoxicating as a shot of whiskey.

However, there were sweeter delights to be sampled when the victim's terror had provided enough sustenance to make the phantom whole. The fuel provided by strong emotions was adequate sustenance, but it was plain bread and water compared to the feast of energy produced by human sexual activity. Licking at the tears that flowed down Cillian's smooth cheeks, the specter savored them like an exotic liqueur. The young man cried out and fought back as his pants were shoved down his hips, but the ghost held him as tightly as a starfish on a mollusk until all struggling ceased.

When Cillian went still, the apparition grasped the young man's wilted shaft and stroked it firmly. Cillian's cock remained stubbornly limp, and a dark smile twisted the ghost's translucent features. When he was stronger, he would be able to control humans without much more than a thought, but for now he would have to do it the slow way.

Cillian squirmed as a clammy finger crept along his crack, but froze again as the icy digit pushed into him. Without subtlety or finesse, the phantom penetrated the hot sheath of flesh and found the bump in the front wall. Cillian whined in protest as the stimulation took effect. Diaphanous fingers tightened around his rising cock and pumped insistently. As the apparition skillfully manipulated him to release, Cillian prayed he had fallen asleep and into a nightmare. He promised the God that he'd only last month decided didn't exist that he would never sin again if he could just wake up with naught worse than a hangover. Unfortunately for Cillian, the only supernatural power in the room had no love for him—only for the essences that his body produced, essences that would give the ghost life… of a sort.

Like a cow being milked, Cillian spurted a healthy amount of cum into the phantom's fist. The pale stream evaporated in mid-air, disappearing completely even as it broke into fat droplets. The ghost sighed and Cillian felt the puff of a weak breath against his cheek. The faint exhalation, redolent of carrion and seawater, frightened Cillian more than anything that had happened thus far. Shaking off his lassitude, he struggled against the phantom that grew stronger with each passing moment. He might as well have tried to move one of the thick columns that held up what was left of the roof. The energy that flowed into the specter surged as the creature absorbed the endorphins the young man secreted. Spiked with adrenaline, the essence of the chemicals spread quickly through the apparition, vitalizing and thickening the wispy stuff of which it was composed until all parts of it were as solid as the arms.

With a hiss, the phantom turned its victim again, pressing close to Cillian's back. The young man cringed away from an unmistakably male organ, aroused and of impressive proportions. The shaft was as cold as the rest of the ghost and Cillian's mind finally fled, refusing to accept what was happening. He was immediately jarred back to harsh reality as he was breached. Without warning or mercy, his attacker drove into him to the hilt, tearing delicate tissues. Blood steamed in the frigid air as it trickled down Cillian's thigh only to vanish before it could drip to the floor.

"Ahhhhh, virgin blood," the ghost whispered.

"I told you he was untried. I've not led him that far down the path of corruption."

Cillian's eyes snapped open as someone walked from the shadows by the stairs, and relief rinsed through the young man at the sound of his man's voice. "Sean," the young man choked out. "Help me."

"Shhh, Cillie," the man said, stopping in front of his suffering lover. "You're being given a great honor. Your life force will allow the great lord who built this castle to rule it once again."

"Help me, Sean," Cillian pleaded, ignoring the words that made no sense to him.

"Of course," the man said, coming closer. Cillian sobbed harder when his lover knelt and kissed his cock. "Hush now, lad. You'll be coming many, many times tonight, and each time his lordship will grow stronger. You'll be drained, of course, but that can't be helped, and there are a lot more strong young men out there. When I've brought enough of them to this castle, the real Lord of Gwarchodwr will return, as potent as he was before he went to the Holy Land."

Cillian screamed as the ghost entered him again. Warm lips closed around Cillian's resurrected erection as the ghost basked in the mortal's horror of the ravishing. The young man's exhilarating fear was laced with the pain of his lover's betrayal, like a mouthful of dark and bitter Arabian coffee. The phantom drank it all in, his power swelling exponentially. "You may go," he told his minion.

"But I can help you, my lord," the man said in surprise.

"You have served me well, but I need no help in this. Go, I tell you, until I bid you return."

Sean obeyed resentfully even as he rejoiced to hear his master's voice so strong and commanding. He had been looking forward to watching cocky young Cillian broken and humbled by the phantom's lust, but even more, he longed to see the expressions on the sheep-like faces of the townsfolk when Sir Alun came into his own again. Sean was respected; people considered him an upstanding, decent man and essential to the community, but he was a fixture they took for granted. That would change when his role as the instrument of Sir Alun's return was revealed. Then they would see what lay beneath his everyday mask, and they would bow before him.

It was only a matter of days before the ancient ritual would be complete and the conjury could be worked. Then the villagers would know what power had slept unsuspected in their midst for all these years. Until then, he must keep his eyes on the goal and ignore small disappointments until the time of his triumph arrived. He never doubted that the scheme would succeed. All that the spell required was suitable donors, and Sean would supply them. He never thought that he was betraying his own kind; he was not one of the sheep. He was a wolf, and a wolf does not pity the prey.

"HAVE we reached an agreement, Sir Rhys?"

Lord Turcotte yawned. "It would seem so, Mr. Red Dog. Once Mr. Andressen signs the contract you're holding, Red Recovery can begin work on the castle."

"My partner will be glad to hear that," Sean "Ardie" Red Dog said, eager to leave his host's condescending presence. With a nod that could be interpreted as a gesture of respect, he rose from the leather wing chair and showed himself out. Once he was in the hall, he flipped open his cell phone and stabbed the top number.

"Bo? Hey, pard—stop your grinnin' and drop your linen. We're in." He paused to listen to his partner's reply. "Hey, have I ever let you down? You sure got that right. Now get your fine ass to Wales and bring the boys. We've got a treasure to dig up."

Chapter One

"WELL, this is just dandy," Bo Andressen said, crushing his paper coffee cup and tossing it accurately at a bin with the legend *cadw Drws Cefnforoedd cryno*. "I can't get onto my own job site. I can't get a decent cup of coffee. I can't even read the trash cans to be sure that's what they are. Gryf?"

"It can't be helped, boss," Hywel Gryffudd answered. "And that is indeed a rubbish bin. The sign says, 'Keep Oceandoor Tidy'. That's a translation of the town's name. You see, the people that settled here in...."

"Can't be helped?" Bo interrupted in exasperation. "Ardie wouldn't say that."

"As big a waste of my breath as it is, I'll point out the very obvious fact that Gryf is not Ardie," James Weir said. "You sent Ardie on a mission, remember?"

With your usual lack of forethought, said the little interior voice that had plagued Bo Andressen all his life. The leader of the salvage team known informally as Red Recovery and formally as the Andressen-Red Dog Recovery Company cocked an eyebrow at his colleague. He'd been taking a lot of heat for sending his partner off before the unpacking had been finished, but Ardie was their scout and knew this place better than any of them.

"I think you should stick to ancient languages, James," Bo said. "You're irritating in all the modern ones."

"You're not annoyed with me," James said, pointing with his chin. "It's himself that's under your skin."

All three Red Recovery employees turned to look at the big man talking to a few representatives of the Welsh news media. The ancient castle on its rocky isle across the narrow strait made a dramatic backdrop for the tiny press conference—not that Gavin Gilroy needed set dressing to look impressive. Tall, well-built, with red-gold hair and the wolfish features of a Saxon raider, Gilroy drew notice. Bo eyed the movie-star handsome policeman sourly. The salvage team had a contract and all their equipment had arrived, but they'd been cooling their heels in this sparsely populated corner of Wales for almost the entire day.

"Shit!" Bo muttered. "Where the hell is the owner? You're a native, Gryf. Can't you do something? Did you try calling Lord Turcotte again?"

The engineer shook his head. "His secretary said he would call us."

"And you believed her?" Bo was incredulous.

"Him," Gryf corrected. "And yes, I believed him. I think we should go to the pub. Hanging around here is going to give you an aneurysm."

Bo's fists clenched. "It just pisses me off. The body was removed yesterday. The police have been all over the damned place like ants. Why can't we get started?"

The flicker of James's eyes behind his rimless glasses warned Bo just before Gavin Gilroy spoke behind him.

"I explained it to your man Red Dog yesterday," Gavin said. "But if you want to have a chat with me, you can come along to the pub."

Bo blinked, turned around, and then held out his hand. "Robert Andressen," he introduced himself. "Folks call me Bo, and I'd appreciate a chance to make my pitch."

"Constable Gavin Gilroy." The policeman introduced himself as he returned the pressure of Bo's hand. "And you don't have to thank me. I'm doing interviews, and I'll want to talk with you."

Bo started to protest that he hadn't even been in Wales when the murder had occurred, but then he changed his mind. Instead, he issued a few orders.

"Gryf, go over the equipment one more time. I want to be sure everything's in optimum working order. James...." Bo racked his brain and ended with, "Help Gryf."

Without waiting to see if Bo was following, the policeman walked up the steep main street of the village of Drws Cefnforoedd. He strode into the Briny Rose public house and slammed a hand on the bar as though it weren't several hours until opening. After a moment, a stout man appeared in the kitchen doorway.

"And what can I be doin' for the local constabulary at this hour?" the publican asked.

"I left you 'til last, Sean Dymock," Gavin said mock-sternly. "Out of respect for the high position you hold in this community."

A white smile split the pub owner's dark beard as he laughed merrily. "Aye, there's no one more essential to a Welsh township than the purveyor of strong spirits. Sit, Gavin Gilroy, and introduce me to your new friend."

"I'll have a half-pint of whatever you have tapped," Gavin said. "One for Mr. Andressen here, and treat yourself as well."

"That's a capital idea, boyo," Sean said, but he didn't move.

"Sorry," Gavin said. "Sean Dymock, meet Robert Andressen. Mr. Andressen's the Yank you've been hearing so much about."

The publican nodded. "Goin' t' find the treasure of Castle Guard, are you?" he grinned.

Bo pursed his lips, not happy to hear that his business was local gossip. "I'm going to give it my best shot," he answered.

Sean laughed. "Can't say fairer than that. I'll be right back with our drinks."

Not until they had all sampled their mugs and declared the dark-brown brew delicious would Sean agree to answer questions. Even then, he wasn't happy about it.

"I have to ask you," Gavin said. "Where were you the night before last?"

"You know where I was. Right here at the Rose."

"After hours?"

"I closed up. Sent the girls home and had a drop, all on me own. Then I dragged me wee ass off t' bed, all on me own."

"You didn't go anywhere near the castle?"

"Gavin, man, why would I do that? Get in a boat and cross the channel at night? For what?"

"I swear I don't know," Gavin said. "But I have to ask."

"No, you don't," Sean disagreed. "Not me you don't. You've known me since you came here, boyo, and you know what sort o' man I am. I'm bein' as courteous as I may, but I have t' tell you, I don't much like bein' questioned like this. Particularly in front of guests."

"I'm sorry you feel that way," Gavin said equably. "But I do have to ask, whether it suits you or not, Sean Dymock. It's my job and all."

"And a damn fine mess you've made of it, haven't you?" the publican said, his face deepening in color at a rapid rate.

"Calm yourself," Gavin said as Bo stared into his mug.

"Don't be tellin' me to calm myself in me own bar, ya Northern bastard!" Sean said as he rose from his chair.

"You're making far too much of this," Gavin said. "Pretend it's a business meeting and just try to be professional."

"Heartless git," Sean said. "I was the one that stood by you when you got sent here and no one else would so much as spit in your direction. Who was it introduced you 'round the pub to the lads with influence in Drws? And this is my thanks? I'm a suspect?"

"I never said you were a suspect," Gavin said.

"You might as well have," Sean said. "Comin' in here with your questions. 'Where were you, Sean? And what time might that have been, Sean? Oh, by the way, Sean, did you rape and murder young Cillian Pryce and leave his body hangin' from the castle wall?' How dare you, Gavin? How dare you!"

"Ahhh, ye gods and little fishes. What's all the bloody racket?"

The three men looked in the direction of the groan. Bo glanced quickly at his companions and saw weary disgust on Gavin's face, but the publican's expression was more complicated. Bo saw recognition, relief, and fondness as a pile of clothing in a corner shifted and reconfigured itself into a young man in shabby garments. Though obviously hungover and in need of a wash and a shave, he was strikingly handsome underneath the layer of grime. Feeling a stirring south of his navel, Bo reflected that it had been some time since he'd slept with anyone. The salvager's thoughts veered sharply away from the glowing afterimage of his last lover. Chris—beautiful, golden Chris—so hard and yet so brittle. Chris was one of the things Bo had traveled so far to forget. Resolutely, the salvager banished the luminous image.

"I forgot Morgan was sleepin' there," Sean said. "I'd best get him a drink before he shouts for it and gives himself a worse headache."

Gavin shook his head. "You cater to him too much, Sean. It doesn't help him."

"That would be my business and none of yours," Sean said as he moved away.

"It'll be my business when I have to lock him up or scrape him off the bonnet of someone's nice new auto."

The publican didn't stop walking, but Bo could tell by the man's posture that he'd heard the policeman's warning. As Sean was filling a mug, Morgan rose to his feet in stages. With a tomcat's ramshackle grace that allowed him to narrowly avoid the obstacles in his path, he meandered toward Bo and Gavin.

"Gigi," Morgan said, putting his palms on the table and leaning toward Gavin.

Gavin pulled back slightly from Morgan's boozy breath, which only made the amiable drunk lean closer. Morgan caught sight of Bo and turned to smile warmly at him. Bo returned the smile, feeling as though he were making a mistake.

"Who's your friend, Gigi?" Morgan swayed slightly as he waited for an answer.

Gavin ignored him and addressed Bo. "One of the charming local folk," the policeman said. "Morgan Idris, town drunk, meet Bo Andressen, visiting Yank."

"I prefer to be known as a disgrace to my family," Morgan said. "What're you doin' here, Bo?"

"I'm excavating Castle Guard," Bo said. "I got permission from Lord Turcotte to search the entire island for artifacts."

"You're the one lookin' for the treasure o' Caer Gwarchod!"

"That's the rumor," Bo said. "Any tips on where I might look?"

Morgan grinned and lit up the room like a gigawatt bulb. "Oh, I like this one, Gigi," he said. "Let me buy you a drink, Bo."

"Do you have any money, Morgan?" Gavin asked.

Sean arrived with a mug of beer and set it in front of Morgan. With a look at Gavin that said things were far from settled between them, the publican went back into the kitchen. Gavin let him go in favor of interviewing Morgan while the Irishman was awake.

"And why would I be needin' money when I've friends like Sean?" Morgan said.

Bo smiled, but the policeman looked far from amused. "You think Sean's your mate because he doesn't cut you off though you've a tab as long as my willie," Gavin said and then sighed heavily. "Ah, why am I wasting my breath on you?"

"I haven't a clue, Gigi," Morgan said. "Now, Bo, as I was sayin', if you were to come to this pub on any night o' the week, you'd find me here, and I would be glad to stand you a drink."

Bo nodded. "I appreciate that," he said.

"If you're through flirting, I've a few questions for you, Morgan," Gavin said. "Do you remember where you were the night before last?"

"I'm sure I was here, but maybe you'd better ask Sean."

"That's what I thought you'd say," Gavin said. "All right then, you can go back to what you were doing."

"You're an unsociable bastard, Gigi," Morgan said.

Gavin Gilroy was out of his chair and had Morgan by the throat before the drunk knew what was happening. Bo was impressed by the cop's speed, strength, and knowledge of pressure points. Bringing his face close to Morgan's, Gavin spoke softly. "I wasn't sure if I liked you calling me Gigi or not, but now I've decided and wanted you to be the first to know," he said. "I don't."

Morgan's eyes said he got the message and Gavin let him go. Morgan reeled back when released and caught himself on the chair behind him. Looking down at his spilled drink, Morgan shook his head sorrowfully.

"That's a sad sight, to be sure," the Irishman said.

"You're a sadder one." A new voice joined the conversation.

Morgan looked up at the doorway and grinned sheepishly. "Mornin', Vicar," he said. "We don't see you in here often enough."

"Mock me all you like, but your days of laughter will end, and soon, if you don't take better care, Morgan Madocs Idris."

Gavin turned in his chair and half-rose to greet the man who approached the table. Bo was surprised to see that the black-clothed minister looked like a college student. The rich mahogany hair pulled back in a long ponytail added to the youthful appearance, but the clergyman's demeanor had all the gravity of Jupiter.

"Constable," the young man greeted Gavin.

Gavin nodded respectfully and gestured toward Bo. "Father Sean Carnes, this is Bo Andressen, the man that...."

"The treasure hunter," the minister interrupted. "I've heard about the excavation. How interesting your work must be, Mr. Andressen. I'm pleased to meet you."

Bo took the young man's warm, dry hand, looking into green eyes as wide and guileless as a child's.

"What does that rather sly smile portend, Mr. Andressen?" the vicar asked solemnly.

"Sorry," Bo said. "I wasn't aware that I was smiling slyly. Just doing my best to be cordial."

Cordial? said the dry voice in Bo's head. *Since when do roughnecks use words like cordial? And by the way, is every other person in Britain named Sean?* Ignoring the voice, which was usually right but seldom agreeable, Bo continued to smile at the clergyman.

"Very cordial indeed," the vicar said. "One hears such terrible stories about Americans, but you're quite charming. Do you suppose I could have my hand back?"

Bo didn't quite blush, but he did drop his eyes for a moment. "Sorry again. Still think I'm charming?"

"Of course I do, and I'm quite used to touching others. Minister is also a verb, you know, the laying on of hands and all that. It's part of my calling to provide comfort. Now, if you'll pardon my rudeness, it was Constable Gilroy I was actually looking for. I need to have a word, if you've time, Gavin."

The policeman's eyes flicked to Bo as Carnes hurried to speak again.

"I don't mind if Mr. Andressen hears what I have to say."

When Gavin nodded, the vicar folded his pale hands on the table. "My work is concerned with spiritual matters," he said. "And in my research, I have had occasion to look into certain books that the Church would probably prefer I didn't. In fact, I'm sure the Church would prefer these books didn't exist at all. Be that as it may, when I saw the lad's body displayed on the wall, I...."

"Displayed?" Gavin said. "Why did you choose that word, Vicar?"

"Because the poor soul's body was left as a sign, an announcement of sorts... and a warning, or so I believe."

"And how do you interpret this sign?" Gavin asked, keeping most of the sarcasm out of his voice.

"It lets us know that a particular type of predator is prowling our area," Carnes said. "And it serves notice that an unholy hunt is in progress. I don't wish to be right about this, but I think you'll see more bodies like young Pryce's."

Gavin paused, clearly coming to a decision before he spoke. "It's about to become public knowledge anyway," he said at last. "So I'll tell you that Cillian Pryce was not the first victim to be found like this."

"I've heard nothing," the vicar said.

"The bodies weren't discovered anywhere near here," Gavin said. "And thus far, I seem to be the only one who has noticed the pattern."

"Then we shouldn't dally," the minister said. "I've a suggestion, and I'd like for you to hear me out before you laugh in my face."

"You want to perform an exorcism, Vicar?" Gavin asked with a half-smile.

"No, indeed, not even if I were trained for such a thing. I urge you to contact the people at this number." The vicar passed a piece of notepaper to Gavin. "I think they can help you."

"What is it?"

"The Ceridwen Institute," Carnes said. "One of the world's foremost paranormal research facilities."

"Paranormal?" Bo put in. "Isn't that supernatural stuff a bunch of horseshit?"

"The people at the institute don't think so," the vicar said. "Listen to me, Constable Gilroy. You think you're looking for a serial killer, a man who can be hunted down and brought to justice, but you're wrong. There is no flesh-and-blood monster out there living a routine existence while he waits for the right phase of the moon to take the life of another young man."

"What is it then?" the policeman asked.

"A revenant," Carnes said.

Gavin and Bo looked at one another with raised brows. It was clear that neither was familiar with the word.

"A revenant is a kind of ghost," the vicar said. "Sometimes a person dies under such circumstances that the spirit is tied to the place where they passed over. Sometimes the manifestation is no more than the semblance of the departed, which might appear at certain times with no untoward effects. However, there are restless spirits who feel they have been taken untimely and unfairly. These ghosts are the souls of those who were strong-willed in life, and they can sometimes reach into our world."

"And kill people?" Gavin asked incredulously.

"Please," the vicar said. "I've not quite finished, and you did promise to hold your scorn until then. Even if you don't believe me, it would be a good idea to call the institute and get someone here who can deal with this phenomenon. If not, you'll have more bodies on the wall and a panicked village."

"I'm surprised you would make this suggestion, Vicar," Gavin said.

"I know my flock," the young man said. "Father Brendan, bless his soul, taught me well before he passed on. If they see a medium walking around, they'll feel a lot better about all of this."

"Superstitious buggers," Gavin muttered.

"Aye, to be sure," the vicar said. "They're mostly fishermen, as you know, Gavin Gilroy. They live close to and at the mercy of the elements. Forgive them their little good luck charms and hexes. I do. The talismans are harmless, and they give the folk peace of mind."

"You're the most reasonable religious person I've ever met," Bo said. "I can't get over the fact that you believe in ghosts."

Carnes smiled. "A Holy Ghost is one third of the tripod that holds up the Church, Mr. Andressen."

Bo did blush this time. "You must think I'm a complete idiot," he said.

"No, indeed. I think that you're probably just a little jet-lagged."

"Thanks for the excuse. I'd like to invite you out to the dig for a tour." Bo glanced at Gavin. "When Constable Gilroy says it's okay."

Gavin looked at the telephone number the vicar had given him. "I'll make a deal with you," he said to Bo. "You call the institute, and I'll let you onto the island."

"What? Why?" Bo asked.

"So I won't be the laughingstock of the shire," Gavin said. "And so you can pay for it, if there's a fee involved. My psychic resources budget is rather small."

Bo narrowed his eyes, but it seemed a small concession, and he reached for the business card. "I'll take care of it," he said.

"Thank you, gentleman," the vicar said as he rose. "I hope I shall see you both on Sunday."

"Hope is a wonderful thing," Gavin said. "Thank you, Vicar."

"Nice to meet you," Bo said. "Don't forget. You have an open invitation for a tour."

"I won't forget," Carnes said as he walked away.

Bo watched the clergyman until he was out the door. When Bo turned, Gavin was watching him with interest.

"A darling man, our vicar," Gavin said archly.

"Very nice." Bo refused to be baited.

"Let's talk about something else, then. How did you hear about the treasure?"

"One of my team members, Hywel Gryffudd, spent part of his childhood here with his grandparents. They told him the story of the Crusader's Trove."

"Gryffudd," Gavin said. "I know the name. Guess I'll be having a word with him as well then."

"Whenever you like," Bo said. "Anything else you want to know?"

"Not at the moment. Go ahead and take your equipment to the castle, but stay away from the entry hall."

"You got it," Bo said. "We'll be in the dungeons for the most part. Of course, we'll be camping on the ground floor, but we'll stay out of the crime scene area. Scout's honor."

"You have a reputation as an honest man," Gavin said. "Don't look surprised. I made a few calls when you arrived. At any rate, I'm going to trust you. Don't make me regret it."

Bo stood. "Thanks. I sense you could've been hard-assed about this and kept us off the island until we couldn't afford to hang around, so I appreciate your fairness."

"I see. I'm not doing you an enormous favor, only what's fair. You must be the world's worst arse-kisser, Andressen."

Bo grinned. "My friends call me Bo," he said.

Gavin nodded. "Okay, Bo. If I had any friends, I assume they'd call me Gavin."

"Good-bye for now, Gavin," Bo said as he left. As he walked outside, Bo took out his cell phone and flipped it open. Punching a number on speed dial, he continued walking.

"Hey, pard, what's up?"

"Listen up," Bo said and read out the institute's number.

"Hang on just a... got it. Ceridwen Institute for Paranormal Studies. Interesting. Thinking of holding a séance?"

"Damn, you're good!" Bo said. "Maybe we don't need this institute after all."

"I don't get it, pard. What's the punch line?"

Bo smiled, picturing Sean Red Dog's slim fingers hovering over the keys of his laptop. "No joke, Ardie," he said. "Where is this place?"

"Canterbury."

"Great. On the other side of the country," Bo groused.

"It's not that big a country, Buckwheat."

Bo could hear the smile in the other man's voice. "Right. If you're finished with your current project, take the chopper over to this psychic place and get me one."

"Say again?"

"Look, Ardie, I don't want any crap about this, at least not on the phone. The local cops won't let us dig until we get a psychic out here. Oh, and we're supposed to let everyone think that this was our idea. *Comprende?*"

"No, not really, but if you want a fortune teller, I'll get you one."

"Never doubted it. See ya later."

"Not if I see you first." Bo's partner completed their good-bye litany and hung up.

Bo flipped his phone closed, happier than he'd been in forty-eight hours. Things could finally get under way, and, if they were lucky, it would go a lot smoother from now on.

I wouldn't bet on it, the voice in Bo's head remarked.

CHAPTER TWO

SEAN RED DOG got out of the vehicle and stood looking at the front of the Ceridwen Institute as the taxi sped away down the wet, leaf-strewn road. The fourteenth-century estate home of pale, ochre stone was not large but managed to be impressive nonetheless with its moat, crenellated parapets, and square donjon tower rising above the walls. There were three expensive-looking cars in the small gravel lot, and one beater with its hood up. Seeing a mechanic leaning over the engine, Ardie approached to learn what he could before going in, forewarned being forearmed. As he reached the car, a hose came loose, spraying the workman's hands and face with some sort of viscous fluid.

"My timing could be better," Ardie murmured.

The grease monkey straightened up in surprise and knocked his head hard on the underside of the hood.

"Sorry," Ardie said, wincing in sympathy as the young man rubbed his head. "I was hoping I could ask you a couple of questions."

The face under the mask of oil didn't look happy, but the mechanic answered mildly, "No worries. I'm not having much luck anyway."

"This is the psychic institute right?"

"I'm not sure if the entire building is clairvoyant, but they train what they call gifted people here."

"Gifted, huh? What sort of gifts?"

"The usual. Telepathy, teleportation, telekinesis, all the tele-somethings, prescience, prognostication, dowsing...."

Ardie nodded, listening with half an ear to the stream of words. A vague sense that he'd met this kid before kept scratching at the door of his memory bank, but it was impossible to tell what the mechanic looked like under the grime and this was Ardie's first visit to Canterbury. It was unlikely that he knew this young man, but the feeling of familiarity didn't fade.

"Are you keen to find out if you're gifted?"

Ardie corralled his wandering thoughts. "Me? No way," he said firmly.

"They give all sorts of tests. I hear they don't hurt at all."

"No time. I just need to hire a psychic and get back to work."

"You should take some time," the young man said. "Before it takes you."

A faint line appeared between Ardie's eyebrows. "Thanks for the advice... I think," he said. "So what're these doctors like? Arvel and Davies. Ever meet them?"

"Dr. Davies is blonde and beautiful and brainy," the kid said. "Dr. Arvel is an ogre, and not the bumbling cartoon kind."

Ardie smiled. "Thanks," he said. "I think I know what you mean. Do you think they'll rent me a psychic on the spot?"

"Do you have a lot of money?"

Ardie pictured the company's expense account dwindling like sand running through an hourglass, but there was still plenty at this stage. "A fair amount," he answered cautiously.

"You'll need it. And don't hesitate to make a point of it right away. The administration really respects wealth."

"Thanks," Ardie said. "Good luck with the car."

"Thanks. Same to you."

Ardie walked into the foyer of the building and heard a chiming, clear and remote, somewhere inside the building. In seconds, a man appeared at the end of the hall and hurried toward him.

"Good afternoon. I'm Garry Arvel, one of the directors of the institute."

"Sean Red Dog," Ardie returned the handshake. "We spoke on the phone."

"Yes, I remember," Garry said. "Come with me."

Ardie followed the man into an office decorated with stark elegance. A tall woman stood from her desk and smiled a welcome as they entered.

"Hello, Mr. Red Dog. I'm Alicia Davies. We're quite informal here, so you may call me Alicia, if you like."

"Thanks. I prefer Ardie to my given name."

"Ardie?" the lady repeated.

"R. D." he said. "For Red Dog. It's a childhood nickname that stuck, but I'm not here to waste your time. I need to hire a psychic, a medium, I guess, or gifted person, if you prefer, and I'm willing to be quite generous," Ardie winked subtly. "Can we make a deal?"

Alicia's lovely face reflected her genteel shock as Garry spoke.

"We're not pimps, Mr. Red Dog. You can't just walk in here and wave cash at us and buy whatever you want. This institute is dedicated to discovering and nurturing those who are a little farther along the evolutionary journey than the rest of mankind, and that is all we care about. Money means nothing to us."

"I see," Ardie said slowly as he realized he'd been pranked. "Please forgive me for being crass; I'm an American. May we still talk about the possibility of hiring one of your people?"

"Sit down, and let's begin again," Alicia said.

"Thank you, ma'am," Ardie said, on his best behavior now.

"I sense you're on your best behavior now, Mr. Red Dog," Garry said. "And you have the demeanor of a man who has been made the butt of a practical joke."

Watching warily as the other man sank into a chair on his left, Ardie said, "Impressive. So you don't just teach—you're gifted yourself."

"No, I'm just a really good guesser."

"Garry, please," Alicia said. "Can we do this without the thinly veiled contempt?"

Ardie smiled at Alicia. "I don't mind," he said. "I'd feel the same way if some stranger walked into where I work and started acting like a jackass."

"Why don't you tell us why you're here?" Alicia said.

Ardie cleared his mind and began the speech he'd fabricated on the ride from the airfield where he'd left the chopper. Bo had given him precious little to go on, but with what Ardie knew of the dig site, he'd come up with something plausible.

"I'm part of a research team called the Andressen-Red Dog Recovery Company. We obtained permission from Lord Turcotte to excavate Caer Gwarchod in Wales. It may not be news to you that the castle is haunted. What we need is someone with the expertise to, uh, channel this spirit, or whatever you call it."

Garry snorted. "This isn't *Ghostbusters*," he said. "We're a school, Mr. Red Dog, not a temp agency. Alicia?"

"Caer Gwarchod," she said thoughtfully.

"It means Castle Guard," Garry said. "Built by a Crusader, if I'm not mistaken."

"You're not," Ardie said. "Sir Alun was a Crusader. His father was retainer to Lord Monmouth and was knighted for bravery when he saved his liege's life. Sir Alun joined the Second Crusade and came

24

home with enough loot to build a fortress. He chose an islet off the Welsh coast that can only be approached by boat."

"Thank you for the capsule history lesson," Garry said. "What does it mean to us?"

"Don't you investigate hauntings, or paranormal activity, or whatever you call it?"

"You watch a lot of films, don't you?" Garry remarked.

"Okay," Ardie said. "I can see that you're reluctant to deal with me. Let me go back to being blunt. If I don't bring a psychic back with me, we can't dig. If we can't dig, we have to go home and absorb the loss of capital outlay while we seek alternate employment. That represents a major setback. I don't know how you're funded, but I can add a substantial amount of cash to your budget. All you have to do is go to the castle and pronounce it safe."

"I'll go."

Ardie recognized the mechanic's soft accent and turned toward the doorway. The young man was wiping his hands on a rag, but his face was still smirched with grime.

"Tris," Alicia said. "We've spoken on many occasions about the rudeness of eavesdropping."

The young man shrugged. "Some things can't be tuned out," he said. "I want to go to Wales."

"Absolutely not," Garry said. "You need a lot more training before you're ready to…."

"I'm twenty-four," the young man cut him off, "not twelve. I know you'll never admit publicly that I've grown up, but you're going to have to stop coddling me some day."

Alicia smiled warmly. "To Garry you'll always be the little boy who took his hand so trustingly the day you arrived."

"This is not the time for sentimentality, Alicia," Garry said.

"Then we must make time for it," she answered. "These are the moments that count, Garry. Something you men too often forget. Tristan is about to take an important step in the journey of his life."

"No, he isn't."

"And how will you stop him?" she asked.

Garry's mouth opened, but no sound came out. Shaking his head, he turned to Tristan.

"I'm going with Mr. Red Dog," Tristan said firmly. "I owe him one."

"Don't be absurd. Tell me why you really want to go."

Tristan looked down at the rug and back up at his mentor. "Because I'm ready to tackle something without you there to bail me out."

The two directors looked at one another, and then Alicia spoke. "Very well. When did you expect Tristan to arrive in Wales, Ardie?"

"I was hoping he could come with me. I have a helicopter at that airfield down the road."

"Tristan," Alicia said, "run along and have a shower, dear, and put together your kit. As soon as you're ready, you can come back here." Tristan was gone almost before she finished speaking.

"I hope you know what you're doing," Garry said.

"I feel this is right for Tristan," she answered. "If it were up to you, he'd never leave this institute, but safe doesn't always equal happy. Ardie, would you like to have a glass of some very nice single malt and some facts about the psychic you've hired?"

"I'd love that," Ardie said, stifling his dislike of scotch.

"But you dislike scotch," Garry said.

"Cut that out." Ardie turned in his chair to face the other man.

Alicia laughed. "Garry's not reading your mind, Ardie," she said. "He really is a very good guesser. Even I could see the little curl of your lip when I mentioned the drink."

"Sounds a lot like the way mentalists and magicians work," Ardie said.

"My, you are on your best behavior," Garry said. "Weren't you going to include con men and grifters in your list?"

"I thought it was implied," Ardie said.

"Gentlemen," Alicia interrupted. "Can you exchange more than ten words without insinuating something about one another? What would you prefer to drink, Ardie?"

Ardie smiled. "I would've declined the alcohol anyway, since I'm going to be flying. If it's no trouble, do you have coffee? Or water would be fine."

"I'll fetch it," Garry said. "I fancy a cup myself."

"Tristan's gift is quite spectacular," Alicia said as Garry left. "He's by far the most sensitive psychic we've ever tested. By the way, we refer to those upon whom this gift is bestowed as liaisons."

"I've always thought that was a pretty word," Ardie said. "I love the sound of French, but please go on."

"Tristan has an affinity for spirits," she said. "Or rather, the other way 'round. The spirits are drawn to him. If there are ghosts in your castle, he'll soon have them out of hiding, and then he can determine what it is that's holding them on this plane."

"And the ghosts will go away?"

"Once the conflict that anchors them is resolved." She nodded.

"Couldn't we just have an exorcism?" Ardie asked.

"Do you have a demon there as well?" she countered.

Ardie chuckled. "I'm showing my ignorance again. If I could ask a practical question: Tristan's kit, how big is it?"

Alicia tried to hold in her laugh, but it burst free. "Sorry," she said. "I have quite the gutter-brain, as Garry is often pleased to remind me, and kit probably doesn't have the same slang meaning in America.

To answer your question, I imagine Tristan will bring one or two bags with clothing and essentials. Why?"

"Well, the chopper's not really designed to carry cargo, and if he has a lot of equipment, I should probably call for a truck."

"No machines, no computers," Alicia said. "Just Tristan and his clothes. That's all you're taking with you."

"And that's quite a lot," Garry said as he entered with a tray. "If anything happens to him…."

"We will accept it and remember that he was doing what he wanted to do when it happened," Alicia interrupted. "That coffee smells lovely; did you bring three cups?"

"I brought four," Garry said as Tristan appeared behind him.

"Tristan," Alicia said. "You couldn't possibly have had a shower and packed in that time."

"I could've," Garry said.

"Me, too," Ardie said, taking the cup Garry offered him. "It's a guy thing."

Tristan dropped his backpack and overnight bag and grabbed a cup. He added two heaping spoonfuls of sugar and a healthy dollop of cream before tasting it. Ardie ignored the desecration and sipped the excellent black coffee as he observed the prankster over the rim of his cup. It did not escape Ardie's keen eye that Tristan in cleaned-up mode was quite a revelation. The psychic had the sort of face normally seen framed on the bedroom walls of adolescent girls, and the feeling that Ardie had seen those delicate, appealing features before tugged at the hem of his awareness.

"We haven't discussed a fee," Ardie said.

Alicia glanced up at Garry. "I think we'll discuss the fee after the job is done," she said. "I assure you it will be fair. You will, of course, pay Tristan's expenses while he's with you."

"Of course," Ardie said. "Well, if that's settled, I'll call for a cab."

"We can take my car," Tristan said. "I can park it in one of the hangars. Ralph won't mind."

"I thought yours wasn't running," Ardie said.

"Oh no," Tristan laughed. "That heap belongs to Alicia. I've begged her to buy another car, but she loves that one. It has a name, you know. She calls it John Thomas."

"Tristan!" Alicia admonished, but her eyes sparkled with humor. "Why don't you take your bags to the car now? That way, Garry can have a few words with you alone, which I'm sure he's anxious to do. Ardie and I will finish our coffee, and then he'll join you." The two men did as she bade them without argument. Ardie was impressed.

"I'm impressed," he said when Tristan and Garry had gone. "You have a very light touch on the reins, but your control is masterful."

"I'm sure I've no idea what you could mean by that analogy," Alicia said. "Drink your coffee, Ardie, and listen. Tristan Lambert is a very special young man in many ways. He's never attended a public school, for instance. It's been private tutors and academies since it was noticed that he was 'difficult'. He's always seen the ghosts, even in his cradle. When he was very small, he didn't know they were spirits and took them for granted as part of his world. However, when he learned to speak and began talking about the 'shiny people', as he called them, his parents couldn't deal with what seemed like madness. They took him to specialists, and at a very young age he was diagnosed as schizophrenic."

Ardie shook his head. "I can't even begin to imagine what it was like to have no one believe you. You'd begin to doubt your own senses."

"That changed when he came here," Alicia said. "He's very bright. He knows he's different and that he'll never have what we refer to as a normal life. However, I would like him to see that he can have a life outside these walls. Am I being clear?"

"Every time you open your mouth," Ardie said. "And for the record, I like him already. He's smart, direct, and has a sense of humor. He'll fit in with the rest of the crew."

"Oh, I do hope so," Alicia said. "It would be nice if he could just be an average twenty-four-year-old man with a job to do and mates to have a pint with when it's done."

"Lady," Ardie said respectfully, "even if he wasn't psychic, that kid could never be an average anything. His looks alone would set him apart."

"He's not...." Alicia began, but changed her mind in mid-sentence. "Tris sees beauty differently than most people," she said. "Not all people, but most."

"Who are the others?" Ardie asked.

"Those born without sight," she said. "The blind must feel to see, and that's akin to how Tris perceives beauty."

"That makes sense, I think," Ardie said. "Anyway, it's not his looks I'm interested in."

Alicia gave him her sphinx smile. "I'm not going to threaten you, as Garry would no doubt like to do, but I will say that I am quite fond of Tristan, and I'd not like to see him harmed. I'd take it as a personal favor if you'd keep an eye on him."

"Absolutely," Ardie said, setting down his cup as he stood. "Anything else I should know?"

"I would just stress once more that Tristan comprehends things differently and to ask that you remember that and have patience with him if he seems to behave in an odd manner."

"As long as his head doesn't spin around," Ardie said. "Good-bye, Alicia. I'm glad to have met you, and I hope I'll see you again."

"Who can say?" She stood and offered her hand. "But I hope that as well."

Ardie took her cool fingers in his and resisted the impulse to brush them with his lips. She'd think him either juvenile or smarmy, and he'd end up feeling foolish.

"Well… good-bye," Ardie said.

"Good-bye," Alicia said as she touched her knuckles to his lips.

At a loss for words for the first time in his life, Ardie nodded to her and left. Garry was walking in as Ardie was walking out of the building, and they passed one another with a glance of acknowledgment. Ardie continued on to the parking lot, looking for Tristan. The sound of a powerful engine drew his eyes, and a moment later a sleek, bright yellow car stopped beside him and Tristan rolled down the window.

"Well, come on. Get in," the young man called.

Ardie put his laptop case between his feet and buckled his seat belt. "Is this a Lotus?" he asked as Tristan let out the clutch.

"Yeah," Tristan said with a delighted smile. "It's the new Exige. Cool, huh?"

"Pretty expensive, aren't they?"

"Bloody expensive," Tristan agreed.

"How much for this one?"

"I've no idea. I don't write the checks; the institute does."

"So the institute is…."

"Well-endowed?" Tristan asked innocently.

"Ceridwen doesn't need my company's money, does it?" Ardie asked.

"Not really, no," Tristan said. "Sorry about the prank."

"No hard feelings," Ardie assured the young man. "So… how fast is this car?"

"I thought you'd never ask." Tristan shifted up quickly, and Ardie looked over at him.

"This is a country road," Ardie said.

"Know it like me own willie," Tristan said.

Ardie sat back and watched the trees whip by until they reached the grass airstrip. Tristan waved at the man in the door of the small office and continued down the row of hangars. Pulling into one, Tristan locked the car and put the keys on one of the front tires.

"In case Ralph needs to move it," Tristan explained as they exited the structure.

"You're very trusting," Ardie observed.

Tristan shrugged. "Might as well be," he said.

Ardie let that one go. "Okay," he said briskly. "Shall we take to the wild blue yonder?"

The young man grinned. "I can't wait."

Ardie got the kid into the chopper and took off. In a relatively short time, they sighted the rugged coast of Wales with its many smuggler-friendly inlets. Tristan seemed fascinated by everything and spent the trip swiveling his head from one sight to another, exclaiming over each new marvel.

"That was fantastic," the young man said as they were climbing out of the chopper.

"Yeah, I guess it was," Ardie admitted. "This is a beautiful country when you take the time to look at it. Now grab your bags, and I'll take you to meet the boss."

CHAPTER THREE

"I DON'T think we should be doing this here," Billy said. The young man was nervous for more than one reason. The first being the stated one: his anxiety over the location of this tryst. The second reason was the tongue that was currently dipping into the slit of his hard cock. He gasped as a spit-shiny finger slid up his crack. "By all the saints, I've never felt nothin' like what you're doin' to me."

In a very short time, the young man came, spurting a stream of seed that was avidly consumed. His trembling knees gave out and he collapsed backward onto a pew as his lover rose to sit beside him. With a big sigh, he leaned against the man's shoulder.

"Merciful Mother Mary! I came so hard I thought I might black out. I was that worried that someone would walk in on us."

"Adds to the thrill, doesn't it, Billy?"

"My heart nearly jumped out of me chest," Billy said. "I still think it's… blasphemy or something to be doin' it in the choir loft."

"No one's going to catch us. The church is always empty this time of day, and it really is exciting, isn't it?"

"Well… yeah, 'tis," Billy grinned slyly.

"And the word you want is sacrilege, not blasphemy."

"You're so wise, Sean," Billy said. "When are you goin' to take me all the way?"

"Do you think you're ready?"

"You've had your finger in me bum and I liked that," Billy said. "I want you to shag me for real, though."

"If you can ask for it, you're ready. Is tonight too soon?"

"No, that's great," Billy answered. "I don't have to work tomorrow. Where will I meet you?"

"I want to christen a new place. Can you get hold of a boat?"

"Of course I can. What do you have in mind?"

"The castle."

Billy looked surprised and then grinned broadly as he rose to the dare. "We'll have to get past the coppers. That'll be a real thrill."

"Aye," his lover smiled back. "I've no doubt it will. Say, midnight?"

"Perfect." Billy turned in the man's arms and nestled a hand in his lover's crotch. "Now, what can I do about this swelling, I wonder?"

In another moment, slurping sounds and soft moans charged the still air of the loft.

THE sun was setting rather spectacularly as Ardie and Tristan crossed the strait. After thanking the constable who ferried them over, Ardie led the young man up the rocky path to the castle. The sound of music grew louder as they approached the top of the path and the smell of cooking meat filled the cool evening air. On a square of AstroTurf, the members of the salvage crew sat on lawn chairs, drinking from dark green bottles.

"Ardie!" shouted the man at the grill.

Everyone turned to watch Ardie and Tristan negotiate the last few feet of the track. Tristan caught his sneaker on the edge of the faux grass and would have fallen but for the hand under his elbow. The young man dropped his bags and caught his balance, turning to look at his savior. Warmth spread from the fingers on his arm to encompass his body in a pleasant glow. A liquid pulse behind his pubic bone made Tristan's eyes widen in surprise as he stared at the stranger.

Ardie turned to see what was keeping the kid. "Oh, I see you've already met the boss," he said. "Here's the psychic you ordered, Bo. How'd I do?"

"Bo thought the lad was your date for the party," Gryf said, brandishing a long fork.

Ardie dodged the tines as Gryf embraced him warmly. "Hey, careful," Ardie said. "So what's cookin', good lookin'?"

"Don't you worry," Gryf said. "James remembered to pack the sawdust steaks."

"Soybean steaks," Ardie corrected.

"Whatever," Gryf said. "So this is the swami, aye?"

"Hywel Gryffudd, this is Tristan Lambert," Ardie said.

Tristan heard his name, but he couldn't look away from Andressen. Neither could Bo break the odd spell that had them locked in a benign staring contest.

Well, he certainly is a pretty one, said the dry voice in Bo's head. Bo smiled. As usual, the voice was right. The psychic was a definite looker. *So was Chris*. Bo's conscience reminded him that his ex was young and drop-dead gorgeous as well.

"Thank you," Tristan said, smiling at a point slightly to Bo's right.

The spell broken, Bo held out his hand. "Careful on those wet rocks," he said. "I'm Bo Andressen. What are you thanking me for?"

Tristan's pretty face reflected bewilderment for a moment before his smile returned, and he focused on Bo. "I'm Tristan Lambert," he said. "And I'm thanking you for saving me some scrapes and bruises, of course."

"No problemo. Come on and meet the boys," Bo said, pulling Tristan along by the elbow.

Ardie and Gryf followed, stopping at the cooler for beer. By the time they caught up, Bo had introduced Tristan to James. Gryf handed Tristan a beer, and the liaison looked closely at the label in the fast-fading light.

"I've never had this," he said, taking a sip.

The team members laughed at the face the young man made.

"It's the local stout," Gryf said. "And it's a little much until you get used to it. Don't drink it if you don't want to. It's not a test of your manhood or anything."

Tristan smiled. "That comes later, does it?"

The young man received another round of laughter and in that moment became, if not a part of the group, at least its mascot. They ate and drank and exchanged little excerpts of their life histories by the light of a couple of Coleman lanterns until the moon rose. Then the artificial lights were turned off and the men sat watching the moon climb the star stair out of the sea.

"I'd like to see the castle now, if that's possible," Tristan said quietly to Bo.

Bo stirred and tossed his empty bottle in a bin. "Sure. We have lights strung up in the work areas. You understand this place hasn't been inhabited in a couple hundred years."

Tristan nodded. "I just want to go inside and see what it feels like."

Bo grabbed a lantern and said a few soft words in Ardie's ear before gesturing to Tristan. "Come on. I'll give you the tour," he said.

When Gryf wandered off in the opposite direction, Ardie raised an eyebrow at James. "Chess?" Ardie inquired.

"Actually, I think he's going for a wank," James said with a straight face.

"Good one," Ardie acknowledged as soberly as James. "Do you want to play some chess or not? I can always play on the computer."

"I think I'd rather just sit here, have another beer, and look at the castle in the moonlight," James said.

Ardie started to get up and find the cable for his laptop, but instead sat back down and opened another beer. For a brief moment, when he raised the bottle to his lips, he felt Alicia Davies' knuckles instead. The feeling that she would be happy to see him sitting and doing nothing was so strong that he looked over his shoulder.

"What is it?" James asked.

"Nothing. I'm being silly, that's all. I know we're the only people on this island."

"I suppose the police might have planted someone here as a sort of stakeout without telling us about it. Speaking of the police... Gavin Gilroy. Never thought I'd meet another man like the boss, but Constable Gilroy reminds me of Bo. Know what I mean?"

Ardie nodded, remembering his interview with Gilroy when the cop had told him Andressen-Red Dog Recovery could not begin operations. It was never a pleasant prospect, relaying to Bo the news that he couldn't do something he wanted to do. Ardie had been glad to do it by radio from the helicopter. He'd not like to be caught in the middle if Gavin and Bo ever clashed.

"Wonder how the psychic's getting on with the boss," James said in the silence.

Ardie shook his head. "Wouldn't want to make a prediction."

Taking the other man's terseness as a cue, James kept quiet, sipped his beer, and studied the fortress by the light of the moon. Ardie sat back in the lawn chair and watched the black waves dash themselves on the rocks in explosions of crystal and quicksilver. Despite Ardie's avowed disinterest, he, too, wondered how Bo and Tristan were getting on.

BO WAS surprised when Tristan Lambert threw an arm around his neck and sought his mouth before they'd gone thirty feet into the main hall, but he responded instinctively. Tilting his head, he aligned their mouths more comfortably and cupped the back of Tristan's skull in his hand. Boldly, Bo drew his tongue along the curves of the young man's sweet upper lip, and Tristan surrendered his mouth. Bo's tongue delved deeper as he slipped an arm around the psychic's back and drew him closer. Receiving nothing but positive signals, Bo slid a hand down to squeeze a firm butt cheek. He knew he was acting like a teenager copping his first feel, but he couldn't seem to slow down.

The salvager's deprived cock hardened quickly, and Tristan made a small sound as the eager erection pressed against his thigh. Bo grabbed both the young man's lower cheeks, kneading firmly as he rocked his pelvis into Tristan's. The psychic's startled whimper became a drawn-out moan that triggered something primal in Bo. Tristan gasped as Bo bit down on his nipple through the sweatshirt he wore. Tristan's fingers dug into the hard muscles of Bo's back as Bo pushed a hand under the waistband of his track pants, wasting no time in grabbing hold of the liaison's arousal and stroking it ardently.

Beneath the storm of pleasure that barraged his nervous system, addling his senses, Tristan still managed to think clearly. He'd recognized that a paranormal force was present when he stepped over the threshold, but even after giving it free rein, he still couldn't get a sense of the manifestation, other than its desire for erotic energy. So this was it then; this was his chance to prove that he could handle himself. Cautiously, the liaison opened a bit more, and a blast of Saharan heat swept through him, searing away rational thought. Feverishly, the liaison groped the American's crotch until he found the man's hard shaft. Wrapping his fingers around the thick length, he squeezed the resilient flesh.

Bo groaned as his balls tightened almost painfully in response. Grabbing Tristan's wrist, he shoved the psychic's hand down the front of his worn jeans. With no undergarment to deal with, Tristan immediately encountered hot, silken skin, and he caressed it eagerly. With a sound of exasperation, Bo unzipped and pushed his pants to his ankles. It dimly occurred to him that his conscience was awfully quiet, but he was thankful that he wouldn't suffer the usual blow-by-blow review of his lovemaking technique.

Turning Tristan sideways, Bo pumped the young man's quivering shaft as his tongue explored the soft mouth. Something like a sob ripped out of Tristan's throat as his cock pulsed in Bo's fist, coating the scarred knuckles with cum. The noise entered Bo's ears, picking up resonance as it coiled in his brain, stoking his pleasure centers. With an impatient growl, Bo shoved Tristan's pants down and bent the lithe young man over the stone balustrade. He fondled the liaison's sculpted buttocks as he worked the tip of a saliva-slippery finger into the puckered opening. Tristan trembled and panted as Bo added a second finger, scissoring the digits, holding open the small port as he spat and used the saliva to slick the head of his cock. With a short, sharp thrust, Bo drove the first couple of inches into the tight passage. Tristan cried out softly, and Bo reached around to take hold of the psychic's drooping shaft. Unnoticed by either man, a drop of blood splashed onto the ancient stone of the floor and was absorbed.

Angling down as he pushed in, Bo gave his hips a roll as he shunted his hard flesh forcefully, but precisely, into the yielding sheath. As if guided, the blunt tip of the thick shaft dragged solidly across Tristan's prostate on the first stroke and each thereafter. Tristan clutched desperately at the cold marble as the tide of ecstasy swept back in, threatening to pull him under. His body had been commandeered, and all he could do was try to stay relaxed and hope that Andressen was quick. Whatever lonely spirit walked these halls was powerful as well as spiteful, and Tristan couldn't wait to study it.

This near-rape was disturbing, but ghosts often sought physical contact with the living, and the liaison was determined that he could handle it.

I won't panic, Tristan thought, as Andressen thrust deeper. *My body is being used as a vessel, a channel.*

Bo shifted balance, changed the tempo of his stroke, and all of the sensations coursing through Tristan's body melded into one. The sexual tension spiraled higher with each pass of the hard cock, each stroke of the hard fist, until it reached its peak. The liaison cried out and shuddered through a powerful climax that lit up every cell in his body and blazed like a beacon for those with eyes to see such things.

UNTIL the light in his eyes died forever, Billy fixed them despairingly on the man who had professed to love him and then abandoned him to horror. The revenant dropped the drained husk of flesh to the stone floor and rose into the air. Throwing his arms above his head, the ghost of Sir Alun Turcotte exulted in the waves of energy he'd absorbed from his victim, energy that allowed him to mesh with the other, stronger source that was such a tantalizingly short distance away.

Sir Alun's tame Eastern magus had taught him the spells that compelled the boy-witch to rut with the yellow-haired roughneck who resembled the Teuton mercenaries of Alun's time. Using the Arab's formulae, the phantom had accelerated the natural attraction between the two souls and induced them to couple so he could feed. Now, he sucked greedily at the flow of potent sexual energy emanating from the aroused medium until he could contain no more. Replete, the revenant froze, translucent arms and legs flung wide, muscles and tendons standing out in rigid relief. Transfixed by the powerful burst of energy as the liaison climaxed, the ghost of the castle's master cycled between transparency and solidity for several long moments.

"By all that is unholy!" Alun laughed as he floated down to light upon the flagstones. "I have never felt such power. *He* is here, my minion: the one who will make me whole. Prepare him well, and when he is ready, we shall see whose will is the stronger."

"You will best him and take him, my lord," Sean said. "And when you have absorbed the life essence of the witch, you will take your natural form again."

Alun tilted his chin up in an arrogant manner, looking down at his devotee with hooded eyes. "And what shall be your reward when I am incarnate?" the revenant asked.

"I live to serve you, my lord. That is reward enough."

"Come closer."

Obediently, the man crossed the space that separated him from his dark deity. Looking up, he waited for whatever use it pleased Sir Alun to make of him.

"You have served me well," the ghost said in a voice that had regained most of its rich resonance. "Never fear that I will forget that."

"Thank you, my lord."

Alun drew a finger down his minion's forehead and nose, tapping the man's lips thoughtfully. "I will need at least one more sacrifice before I will be strong enough to do battle with the witch," he said.

"It grows more difficult now that the corpses cannot be carried off. Blast these arcane restrictions. I don't see why we cannot simply pitch the bodies into the sea."

"That is beyond my knowledge," the revenant said. "But it is folly to stray from the wisdom of the Eastern necromancers."

"It will be as you say. I wish we had the book itself, but I'm sure we may rely on your memory, my lord, and that of the magus."

"The boy-witch's essences must be stirred to a peak before I consume him. Soon, I will need the help of those vassals still under my dominion. Tonight you will say the incantations that will call them forth from their long slumber."

"I will, my lord," Sean said eagerly.

The ghost began to fade like the fog of breath from a windowpane. "Go now. I must conserve my strength for the battle."

The glowing revenant rose to the ceiling and passed right through it as his servant watched in awe. Only when the soles of Sir Alun's boots had vanished from sight did the minion set to work. After arranging Billy's body, he left the hall, making his way unseen to the water and the kayak hidden among the rocks. Paddling strongly, he made landfall in a few sweaty minutes, avoided the police patrol, and hurried home to perform the ritual.

Bo LET go of Tristan's sated shaft and smeared the slippery seed on his own hard flesh. His cock slid in much easier, and Bo allowed it to sink deeper. Tristan's knuckles were white where they gripped the railing as the man drew back to the brink and plunged in, sheathing his full length. The revenant gloated from the shadows of the vaulted ceiling as more blood trickled down the witch's thigh. The smell of the potent, crimson liquid—along with the heady scent of the creature's seed—was a sore trial to Alun's willpower, but he must wait until the most propitious moment or risk losing all. He had waited too long and planned too carefully to stumble so near the end of the race. Satisfied that all was proceeding as he wished, the ghost dematerialized before he did something rash.

Tristan found his voice instantly. "Please," he panted. "Please, just finish."

Jarred from his sensual trance, Bo slowed his hammering stroke. Easing his grip on the young man's hips, he thrust until he passed the point of no return. As he came, Bo pulled his arousal from the tight passage and spurted into his hand. The sweet, slow spill of afterglow was just starting when he realized the kid hadn't moved.

"Everything okay?" Bo asked.

Tristan turned, swiping his sleeve across his eyes. "Yeah. Sorry. Didn't mean to worry you. It was a rather intense experience."

"No shit. I was more than a little surprised."

"Yeah, me too. I didn't expect to make contact so soon." He saw the puzzlement in the other man's eyes. "I'll have to explain later," Tristan said. "Right now, I need to…."

Bo grimaced when the psychic's voice broke and tears spilled down his cheeks. "You're not okay. What's going on here?" Tristan shook his head as he pushed past Bo. Bo yanked his jeans up and followed the young man, taking him by the arm. "Hold on," Bo said. "Don't go running off. You don't know the terrain."

"Please let go," Tristan said softly.

Bo released the young man's arm and took a step back. "Something weird just happened," he said. "I can see you're upset. Why don't you let me call one of the other guys to show you where you'll be sleeping, okay?"

"I can find my own…." Tristan stopped and stared over Bo's right shoulder. "Where did you go?" he said abruptly.

"What are you talking about?" Bo asked. "I haven't gone anywhere."

Tristan focused on Bo again. "Sorry. I'm a little punchy. Just show me my bunk. I'm not afraid to be alone with you. It wasn't your fault."

"Fault?" Bo repeated incredulously. "Look, you came on to me."

"I know," Tristan said. "I'm sorry."

"I'm not sorry… at least I wasn't 'til now," Bo said as they walked. "Look, I'm not generally the type of guy who jumps into bed after a handshake."

"I can see that." Tristan yawned. "Tomorrow, okay?" he said. "I'm absolutely drained."

Bo got the young man settled in the lesser hall, where the team had set up sleeping quarters, and Tristan fell asleep as soon as he lay down on the cot. Bo pulled the kid's sneakers off and turned down the lantern. With a last look at the delicate features smoothed out in sleep, Bo walked away. It had been a hell of a day, but it looked like his sexual drought was over. In fact, it was raining men.

Never satisfied, are you? Bo's conscience chimed in. He shooed the little voice away like a pesky mosquito and went to his own bed. He'd have plenty of time tomorrow to ponder the vagaries of psychics and their libidos.

Chapter Four

SIR ALUN'S minion came to himself on the cold floor and sat up, disturbing the convoluted figure of black wax painstakingly dripped onto the plastic sheeting. He sat up, rubbing at his eyes, groaning as his muscles complained. The grainy light told him it was still very early, but it was Sunday and the church would be busy all day. Methodically, he set about cleaning up before anyone arrived. If he had timed it right, as he always did, he would be able to join the worshippers as they came in for the first service.

Without bothering to don his clothes, he quickly and efficiently folded the plastic tarp and packed it away with the black candles. When he pulled on his long-sleeved shirt, the slices on the insides of his arms were not visible. They had stopped bleeding almost immediately and by this evening would be nothing but faint scars. His pact with the revenant was not entirely one-sided; there *were* certain benefits. Pulling Sir Alun's token from his finger, he kissed the heavy ring and placed it in an inner pocket. He left the sacristy as though he had every right to be there, pulling the door closed behind him. No one locked doors in Drws Cefnforoedd, making his task even easier. No one noticed anything strange as he joined the congregation.

During the sunrise service, his thoughts returned again and again to the ceremony, wondering if it had been successful. He had done everything correctly, from the cemetery to the sacristy, where the holy objects of the church were kept. However, no matter how certain he was of his skill, he would not know if the summons had been answered until he met with Sir Alun again. As the words of the sermon droned on, the minion reflected that it was going to be a long day. Reaching for the inner serenity of a zealot who knows his cause is going forward, he looked around at the complacent flock and smiled tranquilly.

BO LOOKED up from a set of blueprints. Ardie and James were speaking softly, their heads almost touching over what the team called The Big Ass Book, the artifact Ardie had flown to London to retrieve. The Book had been the most difficult resource to procure for this job. It had cost many hours of Ardie's invaluable time, a promise of a share of any profit made from the excavation, and they had to put up with the presence of the site's owner, the present titleholder and direct descendant of the founder. Sir Rhys Turcotte, or prick extraordinaire, to use Ardie's words.

Bo chastened his wandering thoughts. He was sure there were those who held the same opinion of him. Checking his watch, he saw it was seven already and that the site was due for a visit from His Haughtiness in less than an hour. His mind cleared of upcoming business, Bo's thoughts returned to his encounter with the young psychic. To call the episode bizarre would be to damn it with faint praise. Bo still couldn't understand what had come over him. Sure, it had been a while since he'd had sex, but that didn't excuse the frenzy that had possessed him.

Bo looked guiltily around as though expecting to see Tristan standing behind him, but the young man was off exploring the approved areas of the castle. As anxious as Bo was to talk to the kid, he felt relieved that he didn't have to do it just yet. He was a little embarrassed by his Stone Age behavior and hoped the psychic didn't think he was always like that. And why the hell was he wasting time thinking about this right now? "Ardie," Bo called, and Ardie looked up.

"What do you need, bud?"

"Just taking a break. Anything interesting there?"

"All of it," James answered, removing his glasses and rubbing his eyes. "The penmanship is lovely and very clear. The Arabic is in dialect, of course, but fortunately it's one I'm familiar with, the magus variant. Those who called themselves magicians used it to keep their spells secret. The first half is a catalogue of ancient spells, formulae, and other arcana. The rest is an account of the experiments of a magus called Aqil with later additions by Sir Alun. Whether Aqil was a name, a title, or an alias, we may never know, but he wrote very neatly."

Bo smiled at his ancient languages expert. "And what does Aqil have to say in his tidy handwriting?"

"I'll let Ardie tell you," James said, his gray eyes already straying to the text. "I want to find the part that deals with the building of the caches in the castle."

"Don't let me stop you," Bo said.

Ardie came around to sit at the other end of the long folding table with Bo. "Freaky stuff," he said, pulling out his cigarettes and Zippo lighter. Bo frowned, and Ardie put the smokes back in his pocket. "Seems our Crusader buddy dabbled in the black arts. Unless he acquired The Big Ass Book as an investment."

Bo smiled at Ardie's sense of humor. "What's it got to do with the treasure?" he asked.

"The bulk of Sir Alun's treasure was reputedly stolen from a temple, and not a Christian, Jewish, or Muslim one."

"Mysterioso," Bo remarked. "Good thing we've got a medium."

Ardie's full lips curved in the smile that had made Bo's heart beat faster when they had first met, before Bo found out Ardie was straight.

"Is it skill or luck and does it matter?" Ardie recited the Red Recovery team's informal motto. "At any rate, Sir Alun used The Book as a sort of manual. It seems the knight became obsessed with Eastern mysticism, reincarnation, that kind of thing. When he came home from the Crusades, he had this castle built to a specific design and.... Am I boring you?"

"You're soothing me." Bo returned his wandering gaze to Ardie. "I'm jumpy as a long-tailed cat in a room full of rocking chairs this morning."

"You're just excited because His High and Mightiness arrives today. Now don't embarrass us by asking for his autograph or trying to kiss his feet in public."

Bo's lips twitched. "I'd like to laugh," he said. "But I don't think you find his lordship amusing."

"He's a tool," Ardie said flatly.

Bo chuckled. He had only talked to Lord Turcotte once on the phone. Poor Ardie had negotiated with the bastard for weeks, and still had to go back to get The Book after they'd obtained permission to excavate. It was beyond the understanding of a rational person. Turcotte had known from the outset they would need all artifacts pertaining to the castle, but he seemed to delight in keeping them dangling at his beck and call.

"You've already earned your share of the treasure," Bo said. "Man, it's too early for visits from aristocrats with sticks up their asses."

"Tell me something I don't know," Ardie answered. "So how'd you get on with the psychic?"

Bo flinched, and he knew Ardie saw it by the way his friend's dark eyes narrowed. "You know I'm not a kiss-and-tell kind of guy, but the kid came on to me last night and...."

Ardie's eyebrows climbed toward his hairline. "No way."

Bo nodded, his eyes on the blueprints. "Yes, way," he said.

"You hound," Ardie said in an ambiguous tone.

"He was all over me," Bo said defensively. "It was like a wet dream where you're irresistible to all the babes."

"And they can't get enough of your huge cock?"

"Yeah, that's the one. It was like that."

Ardie pursed his lips. "Doesn't add up," he said. "I believe you, pard. It's just that I don't see that in him, and I'm usually a pretty good judge of character."

"I rely on your judgment," Bo agreed. "But it happened. Don't tell the others, okay? They wouldn't be able to resist ragging on me, and I get the feeling Tristan wouldn't appreciate our brand of humor."

"Not a word," Ardie said. "It's weird, though."

"I wasn't going to say anything until I talked to the kid again, but I'm not sure he's all there," Bo said. "His porch light's on and the phone's ringing, but nobody's home."

"You're describing someone completely different than the kid who flew out here with me," Ardie said. "At the institute and during the flight, he was definitely all there."

"You didn't notice any wild mood swings?" Bo asked. "He went from friendly to firecracker hot to weepy to detached in the space of a few minutes."

"Virgin," Ardie said succinctly.

"What?"

"You heard me. What you described is classic behavior for a...."

Ardie broke off as a shout for help echoed off the walls and high ceilings. Bo was out of his chair and running toward the sound of distress before it faded. Ardie was on Bo's heels, with James a few steps behind. The three men pelted down the stairs to the uppermost underground level of the castle. In the harsh light of the clear bulbs strung on concrete screws, they could see that the passage below was empty.

"Who called for help?" Bo yelled as they reached the bottom.

"In here."

Tristan Lambert's voice was shaky, but loud enough to be heard. It led the men to the room they had dubbed the Privy, for the four large holes in the floor near the west wall. The psychic was kneeling in front of the opening on the far right with his arm inserted to the elbow. At first Bo couldn't understand what was wrong with the picture, and then he realized the white thing sticking out of the hole was a hand. Bo's normally strong stomach rolled over queasily as Ardie pushed past him.

"Who is it?" Ardie was saying. "Can you see?"

"No," Tristan said. "I was trying to uncover his face. I wasn't sure if I should try and pull him out since he's obviously… not alive."

"What happened?" Bo asked in his boss voice.

Tristan looked up and saw Bo. Several emotions flashed across the young man's face, like windows on a passing train. With a visible effort at pulling himself together, he spoke. "I was just wandering around, getting a feel for the place, and when I walked past this room, I looked in and saw the hand. It didn't look real at all. I came in to look, wondering which one of you was playing a joke on the rest of the team, but the closer I got…."

Ardie put a hand on Tristan's arm. "It's okay," he said. "You haven't moved him, right?"

"I just tried to move the shirt away from his face. For all I knew, it could have been one of you stuck in there."

"It's an oubliette," James said from behind Bo, who was talking on his cell phone. "The trapdoors are missing, but you can see the discolored holes where the iron bolts rusted away."

"Go ahead, James," Ardie said. "You know you want to."

"The oubliette," James said, talking to stave off his distress, "is a special sort of cell. The only way in or out is through the ceiling, which is covered by a grate. The typical oubliette is a shaft with just enough room to stand up in. The root word is French, *oublier*, meaning to forget. An oubliette was where you put someone when you wanted them forgotten."

Bo ended his call, put his cell phone away, and joined the conversation. "Cops are on their way," he said. "We're supposed to clear the area."

Tristan stood and swayed slightly. Ardie steadied the young man, looking into Tristan's face to gauge the liaison's condition. "You look a little shocky," Ardie said. "Bo, give me your jacket." Without argument, Bo took off his beat-up brown leather jacket and handed it over. Ardie slung it, still warm from Bo's body, over Tristan's hooded sweatshirt. "You're fine," Ardie said calmly. "You hear me?"

Tristan's gaze was fixed on the middle distance, his head cocked as if listening to a phone in another room. Ardie turned and saw Bo directly behind him. Tristan was staring over Bo's shoulder. Peering down the liaison's line of sight, Ardie tried to see what had the kid so riveted, but there was nothing but blank stone.

"Tristan," Ardie said sharply, shaking the young man by the arm.

"He did that last night," Bo said. "Just zoned out. Gave me the creeps." Bo waited for the little voice in his head to comment on his cowardice, but his conscience had been quiet today. Taking Tristan's other arm, Bo helped move the young man out of the dungeon and up to the indoor camp in the great hall.

"I'll make sure the kid's all right," Ardie said. "You go deal with the cops, boss."

"Wouldn't it be better if you...."

"Not at this point," Ardie shook his head. "You and Gilroy connect on a basic level, and as far as I can see, the man can't be finessed."

"How should I handle it so we don't get thrown off the island?"

"Just be you. I figure we're fucked already, so why not be honest?"

Bo nodded and hurried out to meet the police, who were coming through the enormous front entry. Gavin spotted Bo and veered in his direction.

"This way," Bo said without preamble and led the way to the oubliette room.

Gavin went to one knee and peered into the hole. "Billy Nye," he said sadly. "What on earth are you doing here, lad?"

"It's Billy Nye, sir?"

Gavin looked up at the policeman standing next to him. "Yes, Constable Ifans. You sound surprised."

"Well, sir, I saw young Bill as he got off work last evening. He was sharin' a drop with that worthless sot, Morgan Idris. They were sittin' on the bench in front of the grocer's. Billy still had his apron on, but was sittin' there, bold as brass, passin' the bottle with Idris. I gave 'em the talk on public drunkenness and told 'em to take it elsewhere."

"And what time was that?" Gavin prompted.

"Well, you know the grocer stays open late on Saturday night. Lots of folks come in for ice cream. I'm partial meself." Ifans noted the look on his superior's face and got to the point. "It was half-past ten," he said.

Gavin stood up. "Call that forensics team from London and tell them we'll need them after all," he said. "Morgan Idris. Interesting. He somehow neglected to tell me that he bought a bottle of whiskey for Cillian Pryce the night Cillian was murdered." Gavin looked around and abruptly stopped talking about the case. He ordered Ifans to stand guard and pulled Bo from the room. Not until they reached the top of the stairs did Gavin speak. "Who found the body?" he asked.

"Our psychic," Bo said. "He arrived last night, and if you want to talk to him, he's right over there."

Gavin looked in the direction Bo indicated as a pale Tristan took a bite of the chocolate bar Ardie was holding. Bo turned back to Gavin and had what he was sure was a rare opportunity to see the constable caught off guard. Gavin Gilroy was gazing at the liaison like a man expecting a deer and seeing a unicorn in his garden.

"Gavin?" Bo prompted. "You want to talk to Lambert, right?"

"Yes," Gavin said slowly. "Tristan Lambert, isn't it?"

"You know him?"

"Not really," Gavin said as he walked toward Ardie and Tristan.

Tristan looked up from his lawn chair as Gavin neared, his eyes focused on the big cop. For a moment, Tristan sat frozen and then rose to his feet, staring at the policeman in astonishment.

"It's you," he said as he threw his arms around Gavin.

RHYS TURCOTTE looked out the car window at the sullen, lowering clouds and knew just how they felt. Chris Lukos, Rhys's new secretary, inadvertently pulled a hair and the noble lord smacked the handsome man's ear with the inside of his knee. Chris paid more attention to what he was doing, and Rhys settled back. The driver had a clear view of the action in the rear cabin of the limousine, but he kept his eyes on the road for the most part. As much as the chauffeur enjoyed seeing the arrogant assistant humbled, he wasn't going to risk Lord Turcotte's wrath by hitting another bump.

"Wales," Rhys said. "I hate coming here. Why did I let you talk me into this?"

Since he'd been asked a question, Chris let his employer's thick shaft slide from between his lips and wrapped his fingers around it. "Because of all the money," he reminded Lord Turcotte.

"I'm not sure it's worth coming back here," Rhys said as a light rain began to fall. "My uncle used to drive me to the castle every other Sunday. How I hated it. And him. Still do."

"Your uncle's dead, Sir Rhys," Chris pointed out.

Rhys looked down with a sneer of contempt. "Do you really think I don't know that? The old bastard took his time about it too. God, the way he used to beg for his scotch and cigars."

"Which you took great pleasure in denying him, I'm sure," Chris said.

"I took great pleasure in watching him beg, the way I begged not to be taken to the castle. I took even greater pleasure in instructing my valet to accept my uncle's small bribes in return for supplying him with his vices."

Chris looked surprised. "Why, sir?"

"So he'd die faster, of course. You were sharper than this at your interview, Lukos. Instead of talking, why don't you do something useful with your mouth?"

Knowing the bloody working-class chauffeur could see everything, Chris resumed fellating Lord Turcotte. Rhys looked out the window again, the tint making the skies look even darker. A scowl marred his lordship's face despite what Chris was doing for him.

"He changed in the castle," Rhys murmured. "In that wet, dark dungeon. And we weren't alone. Oh no, never alone. I could feel them, crowding around, watching, licking their lips and longing to join in."

Chris sucked harder, bobbing his head like a heavy metal musician, desperate to distract his boss from his nascent dark mood. Whatever had happened to Sir Rhys—and Chris thought he had a fairly good idea what it was—it had marked the man deeply. Lord Turcotte was unfit for human company when he descended into memories of his childhood.

"That's how I knew I was mad," Rhys said, his words ending any further conversation.

The driver turned up the radio, and the big car rolled on toward Drws Cefnforoedd and the ancient pile of stones that still loomed large in Rhys's nightmares.

CHAPTER FIVE

"I TAKE it you two have met before," Bo said wryly, watching Tristan hug Gavin warmly.

Brilliant deduction, Bo's conscience commented.

Gavin turned his head to look at Bo as Tristan raised his head from the constable's shoulder. Gavin's nose cracked against the young man's forehead, and the big man's eyes blurred with instant tears at the sharp pain.

"I'm sorry," Tristan said to Gavin. "What a way to pay you back for saving my life."

"I knew I knew you," Ardie exclaimed. "Tristan Lambert! I can't believe I forgot your name. You were the victim of a kidnapping a few years back."

"More than a few," Tristan said. "I was twelve."

Ardie nodded. "That's right. Your guardians offered the largest reward ever posted in Great Britain. An off-duty cop saw you with one of the kidnappers. He followed you and called for backup. But he didn't wait for it. He went in without a gun and saved you."

"You've a good memory," Gavin said.

"Yes, I do," Ardie replied. "I collect stories of true heroism. I'd like to hear yours sometime. From your POV. And Tristan's too."

"Perhaps," Gavin said. "Tristan, I need to ask you about finding Billy."

"Billy," Tristan repeated, as though it were the name of some country he'd never visit.

"Yes, William Nye," Gavin said. "He moved here about three years ago, I think it was."

"He looked very young," Tristan said.

"He was," Gavin answered. "But no younger than you. What are you doing here?"

"I'm still with the institute," Tristan said. "I came here to...."

"Of course, you're the bloody psychic," Gavin interrupted, smacking his forehead and instantly regretting it. "I'm as dense as wood this morning."

Gavin's radio demanded his attention, and he excused himself. When he returned, he informed them that the forensics team was on its way and that they should stay well away from the area Constable Ifans was taping off. He also told them they could stay at the castle as long as they remained in the big hall until given permission to resume work in the dungeons.

James happily went back to The Big Ass Book and was joined by Ardie. Gryf returned from his expedition to the nearest hardware store and set to building more temporary workstations. Bo picked up a hammer and helped Gryf while Gavin questioned Tristan further.

"I was going to go up to the battlements," Tristan said. "But I went down instead of up. Not because I wanted to, but...." The young man looked shyly up at the big policeman and received an encouraging look. "This castle is haunted," Tristan said. "There are such strong presences here. I went into the dungeon because one of them herded me. And then I saw that hand."

"Still seeing ghosts, Tris?" Gavin said softly.

"I know you don't believe in spirits that don't come in a bottle," the young man said. "But they're real. As real as anything else. And most of the ones that linger on this plane don't like us. They envy us and they lust after our energy, but they're not disposed to do us favors."

"So there aren't any guardian angels, like those New Agers want us to believe?"

"Sure there are, but they aren't ghosts."

"What are they then?"

"They're spirits, just not ghostly ones. They're composed of energy of a different wavelength."

Gavin sighed. "Let's talk about the murder."

"Murder!"

"Billy was killed. He didn't stumble into that hole and break his neck."

"No, of course not. I guess I knew he was murdered all along."

"I'm sorry you had to find him," Gavin said sincerely. "You've had enough trouble in your life."

"Hasn't everyone?" Tristan asked.

"Too true," Gavin sighed again. "I wish you weren't here," he said frankly.

Tristan met Gavin's eyes squarely. "I looked for you," he said. "Garry didn't want me to, but I got Alicia to help me. We found out you'd been transferred a couple of times after you went back to work. I sent you a lot of letters and never got a reply. Finally, I realized you didn't want to see me. That hurt."

"I'm sorry," Gavin said. "But I couldn't contact you. I would only have dragged you into the shite with me."

Tristan's eyebrows drew up. "What are you talking about?"

Gavin's mouth twisted. "Your hero, am I? You want to know what went through my mind when I saw you crossing the parking lot behind that bar with a man you obviously didn't belong to? I thought, 'Bugger it! Why'd this have to happen on my night off? Now I'll have to call this in.'"

Tristan stared silently at the other man.

"Lad," Gavin said. "It was a gay bar, and I wasn't on a stakeout with the other guy in the backseat. As soon as my superiors realized where I spent my nights off, the whitewash began. There was no more publicity over the rescue and they moved me into the country. They didn't quite dare retire me, but they put me in the closet and locked the door."

"I'm sorry," Tristan said.

"I'm not. I'm glad I went after you. If I hadn't, it would have eaten at me all my life."

"Because you're a good man," Tristan said soberly.

Gavin changed the subject. "So you think ghosts killed Billy?"

"Perhaps," Tristan answered. "But not without the help of a human agent."

"Oh good," Gavin said sardonically. "Something for me to do—hunt down the lackey."

"You'll find the killer," Tristan said.

"And you'll take care of the ghost?" Gavin said the first words to come to mind.

Tristan held out his hand. "It's a deal," he said.

"I think you should all leave here, but it seems Lord Turcotte has powerful friends who want this project to continue. I suspect a great sum of money is at the bottom of it."

"I'm just here for experience," Tristan said.

Gavin's radio chirped again, and he rose with an apologetic glance at Tristan. "Excuse me. The crime scene people are here. I'm not a detective or anything, just an ordinary constable, so I've got to run when they call, but I'll talk with you later."

"I'd like that," Tristan said. "I've never thanked you properly."

"How you doing?" Ardie said at Tristan's elbow as Gavin walked away.

Tristan craned his neck to look up at the man. "A little shaky, but I'll live."

"Oh sure, you'll live, but will you enjoy it?"

Tristan smiled. "You have a real knack for lightening things up. Some might even call it a gift," he said.

Ardie sat down next to Tristan and turned sideways in his chair. "So… what exactly happened twelve years ago?"

Tristan looked up and began speaking without preamble, reciting words he'd spoken countless times, the story honed to its bare elements. "The people who kidnapped me never intended to return me. They kept me alive with the intention of cutting parts off me to send to the police, but they were going to kill me whether they got the money or not. Gavin overheard one of them tell me that as I was being led into the building where they were going to hold me. After calling his friends, Gavin went to his car and got the lug wrench. He climbed to the roof and swung in through a window, taking out one guy when he landed, bashing his skull in. He threw the tire iron at the second guy and knocked him out cold. It was the woman who gave him trouble. She came out of the bathroom with a gun. I was tied to a chair by then, a sitting duck. Gavin grabbed me, chair and all, and covered me as he ran. He took two bullets before we crashed into the door and out onto the sidewalk. All I could see were flashing lights, and then the police opened fire. I heard a rumor that the medical examiner took over one hundred fifty rounds out of the kidnappers' corpses. Gavin got a medal, but I recently learned that he also got the shaft. No good deed ever goes unpunished, does it?"

Ardie shook out a cigarette and caught Tristan's involuntary grimace. Sticking the butt behind his ear, Ardie pocketed his Zippo. "That's quite a story," he said. "Doesn't surprise me though. Gilroy's the hero type."

"What type are you?" Tristan asked.

"I'm a scoundrel," Ardie smiled. "You've told that story a few times, haven't you?"

"It defined my life for years," Tristan said. "Alicia and Garry helped me see that it didn't have to, any more than seeing spirits has to. They've been like parents to me. Garry's a bit stern, but he really does want the best for me as much as Alicia does. I wish I could convince them I'm happy."

"Are you?" Ardie's tone was dubious.

"Yes, I am. Not all the time, but more often than not."

"This can't be one of the happier moments."

"It's strange," Tristan said. "It was terrible finding the... Billy's body, but it was wonderful finding Gavin. I'm not sure how I feel."

"Forgive me for mentioning this, because Bo will never be able to. If he finds out I even hinted to you that he told me, he'll be pissed. If that made sense, nod your head. Okay. I'm going to ask you a question. You can answer it or tell me to fuck myself, but I have to ask because I'm what passes for a medical presence in this motley crew. If you were injured, if you were bleeding, say, you'd come to me, right?"

Tristan looked perplexed for about two heartbeats before he answered. "I'm fine," he said. "Any injuries I might have... sustained recently are slight and already healing. I appreciate the concern for my welfare. That sounds sarcastic, I know, but it's sincere."

"And you won't...."

"Say anything to your boss?" Tristan finished for Ardie. "Of course not."

"You don't have to discuss it with me, but you do know you should be using condoms, right?"

"I'm not...." Tristan began before he changed his mind. "Yeah. Thanks, I will."

"Thank you." Ardie's smile faded as he caught movement on the periphery of his vision. "Fuck me! Here's trouble," he said under his breath.

Tristan turned on his chair and eyed the tall man who had entered the hall like visiting royalty, a waspish attendant buzzing in his wake.

"Excuse me," Ardie said. "I have to meet and greet Lord Turcotte. See you later."

Tristan smiled as Ardie walked away from him. The liaison glanced at Lord Turcotte and his spirit recoiled from the bleak bitterness in the gray eyes. Tristan looked away, and his gaze met that of Turcotte's companion. The psychic flinched away from the disdain in the other man's expression. Turning quickly, Tristan wondered what he could have done to make someone who didn't know him despise him on sight. Were his differences somehow visible to certain people, the way spirits were to him? Did Turcotte's assistant see him as a freak?

Tristan shook his head, physically shaking off the negative thought. He was a gifted liaison. He could communicate with spirits. He could determine what their anchor was. He could break the bonds that held them chained to this plane. He helped them move on and find peace. He silenced the reminders of his odd possession the night before and the way Andressen's spirit guardian had vanished and reappeared only after the manifestation was over. Rising from the chair, the young man draped Bo's leather jacket across the back of it, walked to the impressive sweep of the double staircase, and began ascending.

"WHAT sort of operation are you running here? Your usual cowboy-style, barely controlled chaos?" Chris snapped at Ardie.

Ardie raised an eyebrow and decided it was not a day for diplomacy when Bo's ex-lover showed up at a work site. "What sort of operation are we running here?" he repeated. "I'm sorry, did I hear you right? Did you actually utter that banal and vapid cliché? What's next? Are you going to tell me that I'll never work in this town again?"

Rhys's gaze was as unperturbed as an iguana on a sunny rock as he broke off his visual cataloging of the room and looked with interest at the man who had cooled Chris's jets so effectively.

"Lord Turcotte expected that you or someone suitable would be waiting with a boat to bring him over to the island," Chris complained. "Instead, the police accosted us and our business was inquired into. We had to rely on them for transportation."

"I fully intended to be there to meet you," Ardie said. "Unfortunately, a dead body turned up this morning, and I was detained by the police myself. Can you give me some idea how much more time we'll have to waste in the browbeating and requisite groveling before your boss's dignity is restored?"

"Once a prick, always a...."

"Chris, heel!" Rhys interrupted.

Ardie's heart was warmed by the quickly veiled look of wounded malice in the secretary's eyes as he was called down. He was over his surprise at Lord Turcotte's recent addition to his staff and was spoiling for a scrap with the gorgeous waste of protoplasm who had broken Bo's heart. This satisfaction had been a long time coming.

"Lord Turcotte, what a pleasure to have you visit," Ardie said smoothly. "Not much to see. We're just getting started, of course. Those inconvenient murders have really set us back."

"Save your sarcasm for people like Chris who can still feel the sting," Rhys said. "Fuck, I hate this rotting pile of rock."

"Actually, this structure is in very sound shape," Gryf said as he joined them. "The builders did an exemplary job. Some of the techniques used were very uncommon, unknown even, in twelfth-century Wales."

"Family tradition says the blood of virgins was mixed with the foundation," Rhys said.

Gryf was temporarily rendered speechless by this mental image, and James Weir arrived to take up the baton.

"How very Arthurian of your ancestor," the medieval expert said. "Although, I believe in that particular tale, King Vortigern needed the blood of a child with no father to mix with the foundation of his sinking castle. I suspect your family tradition is the same sort of superstitious nonsense."

"You really think it's just superstitious nonsense?" Rhys said. "That *would* be nice."

TRISTAN walked out onto the battlements and leaned into one of the notches meant for archers. To his left, the jewel-case green velvet land of Wales; to his right, water like a burnished sheet of beaten silver. He could hear the plaintive cries of the gulls that drifted along the face of the cliff and his nose was full of the lachrymal tang of the sea. The sun was very warm on the top of his head as he leaned farther out into the updraft of air. As he gazed toward the village, the wind played with the ends of his hair like an unseen lover. Time seemed to hang suspended like motes of dust in a sunbeam.

On the road to the castle, Tristan could see two men on horses, dressed for a Renaissance Faire in tunics, leggings, and cloaks. One was dark, hawk-faced, and handsome, astride a gray Arabian, his hair like ink against his red tabard. The other rode a chestnut charger but was of a size to make the warhorse seem a steed of ordinary stature. Though neither wore armor, it was plain by their bearing and the broadswords strapped to their saddles that they were knights. Leaning even farther out, Tristan realized he could see some of the landscape *through* the riders, and his features scrunched into a frown. He flinched as a pair of large hands clamped around his hips, a heavy body pressed him against the merlon, and a rich voice spoke in his ear.

"You see Sir Richard and Sir Odilon, who have answered the call."

The deep, vibrant voice sounded like Sir Rhys's, but Tristan had only heard his lordship from across the hall. The psychic could feel what was unmistakably a hard cock pressing against his buttocks, but he was held fast, however hard he tried to struggle. He shuddered when the big hands left his hips to pinch his nipples through his sweatshirt. Cold lips moved against the nape of his neck, raising goose bumps over his whole body.

"How I wish I might take you now and spill your blood on these stones again."

Tristan moaned in distress as he was rocked hard against the crenel. Cruel fingers tangled in his hair, yanking his head back, exposing his throat like a sacrifice on an altar. A sullen heat built in Tristan's groin as he was held down and caressed against his will. *Get a grip*, he told himself angrily. *You're possessed again.* Tentatively, the liaison unfurled the link that was his gift. As soon as the conduit was open, Tristan felt the presence pounce and lock on. Expecting this reaction, he did nothing that would feed the ghost. Serenely, Tristan waited for the spirit to act again. Instead, it rose and dissipated like mist when the sun comes up.

Tristan braced himself against the cool stone, waiting out the shaky stomach and jelly legs before he opened his eyes and looked down again. As he expected, there were no horsemen. They belonged to the very distant past, as did the persistently randy spirit who had assaulted him again. The next time they met, Tristan was determined to gain the upper hand and discover the revenant's purpose. He would start actively hunting the ghost as soon as he got his breath back.

Chapter Six

TRISTAN walked carefully down the steps to the first underground level, intent on luring the revenant. The rock was damp down here and sometimes patches of wetness accumulated, making footing treacherous. The only light was provided by strings of bare bulbs temporarily attached to the walls, and the pathways were bordered by swathes of impenetrable shadow. The liaison was relieved when the tapping noises turned out to be one of the crew chipping at the seam between two stone blocks.

Gryf nodded cordially but didn't stop working as Tristan passed him to take the narrower set of stairs that led to a lower level of dungeons. According to James's research, it was here that prisoners had been interrogated, and traces of ancient devices of torture could still be found. Tristan touched a hesitant finger to a flaking iron ring bolted to the wall and shivered at the thought of some unfortunate chained in the dank darkness, suffering and despairing. A tear overflowed and ran down Tristan's cheek to drip from his chin and hang suspended in the flaring torchlight. Tristan stood still as stone, caught between one moment and the next as a big man in a cloak like shadows caught the shimmering droplet on his forefinger. Raising it to his lips, the ghost sucked the salt water from the end of his finger.

"There is no vintage so fine," the specter murmured. "And you are such a fool."

The vibrant voice sent a shock wave though each cell of Tristan's body, jarring him from his trance. It was the presence from the battlements, the same spirit that had commandeered his body on his first night in the castle. The manifestation was the most tangible the liaison had ever encountered, and he saw now that he should have been more cautious. He had come down here like a schoolgirl going to pick daisies, but the ghost now displayed power to rival his own. This was not going to be a simple matter of outlasting the pranks and ploys of a petulant home-haunter until he had a good enough metaphysical grip to deploy the link. In fact, Tristan wasn't sure how he was going to deal with this. Already the revenant had taken control of sections of his psyche like a virus in a hard drive.

Memories of a past that was not his own barraged him.

Long vistas of burning sand rippled beneath a sky with the color baked out of it. Hordes of dark-robed enemies screamed the name of their deity as they ran forward. Flesh yawned open to spray his face with a red fountain as his sword cleaved a path through the slaughter.

The incense-laden gloom of a holy place. The din and clangor of battle outside the door. Gauntleted hands held a slender, struggling figure on an ancient altar. The thrust and the spilling of blood.

Torchlight glinted redly on wet walls of rough rock. Iron chains clanked rhythmically against stone. A captive groaned in utter travail of flesh and spirit.

Tristan's vision cleared, and he saw that the rock walls of the vision were those that surrounded him now. The ruddy light of torches in bronze cressets replaced the stark electric illumination. The manacles looked freshly forged, eager to sink their cruel clutches into soft flesh. Ugly, blackened metal implements lay across a brazier that glowed with red-hot coals. *Steady on,* Tristan thought. *None of this is real. No more real than the vision you saw from the battlements.*

However, he remembered vividly the cold weight of the body pressing him against the sun-warmed stone of the parapet. The sensation of being dry-humped had been quite convincing, and the earthy euphemism helped Tristan get a leash on his runaway imagination. He had been in similar situations before, albeit with Garry or Alicia at his side, and he had a fair amount of practical experience. He knew that many apparitions were strong-willed enough to make a psychic see things as the spirit wished them to be, their longing for the past so fierce it had a life of its own. In each of those cases, however, there had been only one scenario, and it never varied. It was always the ghost's idealized image of the past or an endless re-creation of the apparition's death. Whoever was haunting Caer Gwarchod was powerful and cohesive enough to create multiple mirages, and Tristan was simultaneously apprehensive about confronting a spirit of such potency and excited at the prospect of learning more about it. As far as he knew, this was the most impressive manifestation in history.

Reassuring himself of his own esoteric gifts, Tristan conquered his fears and exerted his will. The horrible tension of the "on hold" feeling broke like a rubber band stretched to its limit. Having released himself from the odd paralysis, Tristan deployed a method unique to him, the one Alicia dubbed "quicksand." Allowing his link to bloom outward, Tristan let the arcane energy settle to cover him like a mist. When he visualized it, he pictured tiny motes of silvery-purplish light in a dancing fog. Cloaked in his gift, Tristan waited for the ghost to make another move so he could draw it in. He had time. He could be patient. The important thing was that he wasn't afraid.

"RIGHT here." James tapped a spot on the blueprints.

Bo rubbed his chin, calluses catching on two days' worth of golden stubble. "Of course it would be in the dungeon," he said lightly. "Where else?"

"I didn't say that this was the trove," James cautioned. "Just that something was hidden here, an object that the magus considered a token of great power. I'd wager my share that it's the key to finding the treasure. Aqil refers to it as *Al Clavo*, an amalgam of Arabic and Spanish that means The Nail. Loosen your sphincter, lad. It might not be an actual nail and probably not one from the True Cross. It's even possible I've mistranslated, since clave means key, but I don't think so."

"Shit, another dream of glory stomped on. What do you think it is, Jamie?"

"Probably a dagger, stiletto, or misericordia, something of that nature. The sort of blade that was used to give the coup de grace to the mortally wounded, and if you persist in calling me Jamie, I shall procure one and use it on your pathetic manhood."

Bo shrieked in a comic falsetto and covered his crotch with both hands. Lord Turcotte looked over at the group around the table and said something to Ardie. Bo caught sight of Turcotte's companion, did a double take, and spoke quickly.

"Someone should go check this out right now," Bo said. "Is that the map of the location?"

James looked surprised when his boss snatched the paper from his hand. "Yes, it's on the second level. The map isn't perfectly accurate. Make corrections while you're there."

James was puzzled by Bo's hasty departure until he made the acquaintance of Lord Turcotte and his secretary. His respect for his boss's knack of avoiding unpleasantness went up several notches.

"CLEVER witch," Alun said, using some of the precious power he'd stored up to make himself more solid. "I have never encountered one such as you. You are not afraid of me, are you?"

Tristan almost answered, but remembered to hold his tongue. Let the spirit declare itself and reveal as much as possible before giving the ghost any power over oneself by imparting knowledge. Garry had cited this guideline on more than one occasion. If Tristan had followed procedure instead of thinking he could make his own rules, this would probably be over already.

"It does not matter," Alun said. "Speak or stay silent as it pleases you. I shall still take your essence to give me the strength to break the bonds of death. The rightful lord of this place shall once again hold sway here. "

A cold finger ran the length of Tristan's spine. He had been threatened before, but always he had known the threats to be empty of serious danger. This ghost exuded such menacing self-confidence that Tristan's faith in his ability to banish the revenant was shaken. He should have realized right away that it was the ghost of the Crusader who'd built this castle.

"Tremble, little one," the phantom lord said. "Though it does not show on your face, your insides are quaking. Did you like what I did to you on the parapet? Do you yearn now for my touch, slut that you are?"

Tristan steadfastly kept his lips closed and drew his gift around him like a blanket to keep out the cold evil that radiated from the apparition.

"You burn to feel my touch again," Alun said. "I can see it in your eyes, as I saw it then, the same heat that burns in the black eyes of the Saracen houris. You were born to bear a warrior's weight and take him with you to paradise."

Alun moved purposefully forward and Tristan took a step back. Realizing how far he'd gone into the ghost's fantasy world, Tristan tried to see the dungeon as it really was, but no matter how hard he concentrated, the torches still burned stubbornly bright. Though he knew that none of this could possibly be real, Tristan found he was retreating until his back was against the wall.

"Pretty one," Alun said, looming over the young man. "You cannot escape your fate."

In sudden panic, Tristan focused the mist into a shield-shape and pushed it at the ghost. Sir Alun was flung across the dungeon, passing through the far wall and out of sight. The young liaison stood with hands braced against the damp stone behind him, staring, wide-eyed and panting, at the spot where the phantom had disappeared. Tristan had sworn not to use his gift offensively, except as a last resort, and though he'd felt threatened, he wondered now if he hadn't overreacted. When nothing happened for several heartbeats, Tristan drew a deep, shuddering breath and stepped away from the wall as a ghost with the face of a Bedouin prince appeared in the doorway.

"Forgive me," the phantom said. "I cannot allow you to leave."

Tristan was slow to react as the dark-cloaked figure flowed into the room. Cobra-quick, the ghost snaked out his hand, gripped the young man's throat, and applied firm pressure. The spirit's fingertips sank into Tristan's flesh, and the liaison stopped moving. Tristan fought panic as his gift went dormant and refused any attempt to rouse it.

"Again, I must apologize," the ghost said. "It is not by my will that I do this, but that of Sir Alun, may his name be forever cursed."

"Aqil is not a very respectful servant," Alun said as he re-materialized. "But it would be impossible to do this without him."

Tristan stared at the Crusader's ghost in dread. The situation had changed dramatically. There was no longer a buffer between him and the Unseen World.

"You may as well speak, witch," Alun said. "Your powers are checked by the magus's magic. Aqil, bring him here to me."

Aqil released his choke hold and marched Tristan to Alun. Two more ghosts appeared at Alun's shoulder, both as tall as he and with the same martial bearing. The three knights stood over the liaison like tigers surrounding a staked lamb, while the magus hung back.

"Why are you doing this?" Tristan spoke at last.

"To prevent brigands from taking my treasure," Sir Alun said.

"You've remained on this plane for nine hundred years to guard your treasure?" Tristan asked. "Surely you have a more compelling reason than that."

"His soul is bound to the precious things he took from the temple," Aqil answered before Alun's glare silenced him.

"I will take you, witch, and consume your essence," Alun told Tristan. "And I shall be reborn into flesh. Then I will taste the wonders of this new world. "

"Impossible," Tristan breathed.

Alun laughed and leaned back against the broad chest of the ginger-haired knight. "I do not care what you believe to be possible, little one."

"He is a toothsome morsel," the big man said. "When may we sample him?"

"Patience, my lusty lion," Alun grinned. "The feast is not yet prepared, but since he was foolish enough to invite us, we may enjoy certain delicacies while we are waiting."

Aqil's kohl-rimmed eyes burned with contempt, but his soul was in thrall to the lord, and he could not disobey. Reluctantly, the Easterner prepared the gifted one, salving his qualms with the knowledge that it would make the ordeal easier for the young man, as well as serving Alun's purpose.

"Softly, Doe-Eyes. I will not cause you pain," Aqil told Tristan.

The liaison whimpered as a strong pulse of erotic electricity galvanized his groin. He felt his cock rise like a magic rope trick, stretching the crotch of his track pants. The slight pressure of the fabric on his erection was maddening as the waves of pleasure ratcheted ever higher by the second. He felt as though he were going to climax when Aqil spoke.

"The offering is prepared."

BO GAVE vent to a vicious curse and slammed his fist against the wall at the top of the stairs. The skin of his knuckles broke open and began to bleed, but he didn't notice. *Chris. What the fuck was Chris doing here?*

Tormenting you, of course, the little voice said. *After all, it's all about* you, *right?*

Chris is working for Turcotte, Bo argued with himself. *He knew I was here. This is deliberate.* Bo's conscience seemed to have no answer for that. It was unfathomable to Bo that Chris would come home to England and accidentally take a job with the man who owned the castle where Bo was working. It had to be a plot to torture him further.

It was almost a year since Bo had last seen gorgeous, exciting, and very skilled Chris, and it appeared as though none of Bo's wishes had been granted. Hideous boils had not erupted all over the blond man's face and body, nor was he walking as though a surface-to-air missile was lodged in his ass. Chris was just as gorgeous as the day he'd walked away from Bo, and he probably had Turcotte wrapped around his pretty cock.

Why me? Bo wondered.

Because you're cursed by the gods, his conscience said. *Must I keep reminding you?*

Shut up, Bo suggested darkly as he continued down the stairs.

SHIVERING with unbidden lust, Tristan sagged and was caught by the biggest knight. The liaison was appalled by the solidity of these ghosts; even in their shadow realm they should not be capable of such physical acts. The arm around Tristan's chest and the big hand that ensnared both his wrists felt all too real as Sir Alun peeled Tristan's pants down his hips far enough to expose the rosy head of his arousal. The Crusader's ghost squeezed, and a pearl of fluid welled from the tip. Alun painted the red-haired ghost's lips with the viscous essence and Richard's tongue flicked out to savor the taste.

"What of me?" the third ghost inquired silkily.

"Come, Odilon," Alun invited, moving aside.

Odilon removed Tristan's pants and lifted the liaison's calves to his shoulders. Wrapping his arms around the long thighs, Odilon buried his face in the young man's crotch. Tristan jerked spasmodically when the ghost's cool, slippery tongue slid into his anus. The slick muscle felt longer than it should have as it probed into Tristan's sheath. The rough/soft tongue tip nudged Tristan's prostate and swirled around the sensitive bump. Aqil watched in disapproval, his tattooed lips moving in a silent incantation that sustained the young man's unnatural arousal. It was an unworthy use of the magic, but the magus could not disobey his master. When the corrupt Crusaders had slaked their thirst, Aqil would give the favored one the solace of forgetfulness, wiping this rape from his memory.

"How does he taste?" Sir Alun asked his minions.

"Like life," Odilon answered.

"Like victory," Richard declared.

Tristan shuddered as Alun took hold of his aching manhood and pumped it firmly. Richard leaned over the stiff rod of flesh and lapped at the salty liqueur it produced. Tristan squirmed between them, moaning helplessly in the throes of a terrible bliss as the knights absorbed the emanations of his distress.

"Sublime," Odilon commented, licking at Richard's lips.

Alun nodded a command and Richard took Tristan's length down his throat without hesitation. Odilon tongued the young man's tightened scrotum as he pressed the tips of his thumbs to the furled rosette below. Richard engulfed the young man's pulsing rod to the root, swallowing as he let it slide between his lips. Rubbing another talisman in his fingers, the magus magnified the arousal spell, speeding the buildup of release. While connected to the youth by the spell, Aqil let the waves of energy radiating from the gifted one wash over him and revitalize him. It was not strictly honorable, but he needed to stay strong.

Tristan twisted in the grip of overwhelming sensation. Richard's teeth scraped at the swollen vein on the underside of his cock while

Richard's mustache tickled the drawn-up sac below it. Odilon's tongue teased the sensitive skin around the liaison's opening while he massaged the tingling nub of his prostate with two fingers. Tristan gave a muffled cry as the first precursor of his climax pierced his groin with a dart of intense pleasure. Richard sucked harder, savoring the delicate flavor of the hot, silken flesh. Odilon stabbed his tongue into the psychic alongside his fingers, and Tristan cried out again as his cock twitched against the back of Richard's throat. Sir Alun poised himself to receive the outpouring of energy when Tristan reached his peak. Aqil touched a silver charm at his neck and prayed to a Goddess who had long ago turned Her face from him. *Dark Mother, keep this innocent child from harm.*

"Who's fucking around down here?" Bo called out.

"Damn the man!" Alun cursed, lifting his head. "Aqil! Have we time?"

"He is very close, Lord," Aqil said ambiguously.

"Saracen trickster," Odilon said, rubbing harder at the young man's trigger. "Make him spurt."

"You know I can only influence him, Lord," Aqil said with satisfaction.

Tristan groaned loudly, and Bo called again from outside the door. Sir Alun made an inarticulate sound of rage, and Odilon pulled his fingers from Tristan's sheath. They would have to try again later. Grabbing a fistful of his knights' hair in either hand, Alun pulled them with him as he ascended.

"Learn to suck a cock," the revenant snarled at his minions as they faded in mid-air.

Aqil rose to join them, and they disappeared from sight as Bo entered the torture chamber.

CHAPTER SEVEN

MORGAN IDRIS, nobody's favorite son, was dead drunk and snoring loudly with his head on a stout oak table in the Briny Rose. Ah, but in his dreams he rode across the velvet hills of Eire on a giant stag as white as snow with an ebony rack of many points. His tunic was so richly dyed it glowed red as poppies even in the moonlight. Thick, dark hair was held back from his face by a golden band and gathered into a braid that reached to his belt. In the crook of his left arm he cradled a harp, and with his right hand he coaxed sublime melodies from the silver strings. As the stag ran, Morgan sang in ancient Celtic of a land where poets and warriors were honored and mead flowed like water in halls of gold.

The mythic animal brought them to a chalky path between two parallel rows of tall flame-shaped trees. The narrow, dark green leaves were crushed beneath cloven hooves, releasing the ancient perfume of sandalwood. Ahead was a fountain of black marble, before which stood a tall woman clothed in white. She lifted her head, tresses as red as Morgan's tunic flowing like blood down her alabaster breasts and shoulders. Beckoning to the harper, the lady crowned with apple blossoms smiled in welcome. Morgan began to dismount when she held up her hand.

"You must go back, my champion," she said, in a voice sweeter than the scent of honeysuckle. "I bid you return to the Waking World and defend your brother."

"I have no brother, Lady, as you know."

"Not a brother of the flesh, but of the spirit. Go now in sweet forgetfulness, my hawk. You may return when your task is finished."

Morgan woke and sat blinking blearily at the convivial crowd that filled the pub. Out of habit, he picked up the mug in front of him and brought it to his lips.

"Strewth! Watch it, mate!" a passer-by exclaimed as Morgan spit out a mouthful of beer and a cigarette butt.

Ignoring the annoyed patron, Morgan surged to his feet. From behind the bar, Sean Dymock watched his most loyal customer lurch for the door as if he had a purpose. A frown corrugated Sean's forehead as he glanced at the clock. It was nearly closing time, and he called for last orders so he could be about personal business.

Bo ENTERED the dungeon just as Tristan's limp body hit the floor and the young man yelped in pain. Stuffing James's map in his pocket, Bo hurried across the room. As he knelt beside the liaison, he took out his radio.

"Hey Ardie, what's shakin'?" he said, code for, "Is anyone with you?"

"All clear," Ardie said. "Scraped Sir Rhys off on Gilroy. Fuck, can you believe Chris's nerve in coming here? What a piece of work."

"Ardie, I need you to come to the torture chamber right now. Bring your first-aid kit; we might need it."

Bo's second-in-command didn't stop to ask a lot of questions. He merely gathered some essential facts as he walked over to his partitioned area and grabbed his bag. Who was injured? What was the nature of the injury? Was he conscious? Bo answered, but Ardie didn't know much more than he had before he'd asked the questions. Bo put his radio down as Tristan started to shiver. Putting his wrist to the young man's forehead, he felt for inordinate heat, but even though Tristan looked like he had a fever, his skin was cool to the touch.

"What the hell were you doing?" Bo murmured, assessing the psychic's pants-less state. "Pulling your pud in the dungeon?"

Having been granted forgetfulness but still under the spell of arousal, Tristan moaned at the man's touch. Blindly, he reached out and grabbed a handful of male crotch. Having found what he craved, Tristan squeezed enthusiastically.

"Oh shit," Bo breathed. "Not again."

"Please," Tristan whimpered.

Bo swallowed hard. He cut his eyes to the door and then back to the young man pitifully begging him for release. *What the hell are you thinking?* Bo's conscience spoke up. *You know this is wrong.* Bo ignored it. The echoes of the Saracen's erotic magic resonated in his groin and shut down the rational parts of his brain.

"I'm probably damned already anyway," he muttered as he gripped the young man's arousal.

Tristan did all the work, thrusting quickly into the man's hand until he shot a powerful stream of seed into the stale air. With a sigh of relief, the young man settled to the floor and closed his eyes. Focused on the psychic, Bo didn't see the cum evaporate before it could fall to the floor.

Feel good about yourself? Bo's little voice began to berate him.

"Bo!" Ardie called, drowning out Bo's guilty conscience.

"In here," Bo called back.

By the time Ardie came through the door, Bo had pulled up Tristan's pants and was taking his pulse.

"Let me," Ardie said, gently but firmly pushing Bo aside.

Tristan immediately latched on to Ardie's crotch. Ardie recoiled so fast he landed on his butt.

"Whoa!" he remarked. "What the hell was that?"

"I tried to tell you," Bo said. "He does that."

Ardie eyed Tristan warily as the young man whimpered and stretched out a hand in supplication. "Uh, this is weird," Ardie said. "Is there a male form of nymphomania?"

"Why are you asking me?"

"Just wondering aloud," Ardie said. "Man, look at him."

"I don't dare," Bo said. "It'll make my dick hard."

Ardie glanced at Bo's crotch. "Too late," he said. "Want to hear something really weird?"

"Weirder than this shit? No, thank you. This is plenty weird enough for me."

Ardie's lips twitched. "I'm not gay, a fact you're well-acquainted with, but right now I've got a raging, throbbing hard-on right out of a cheesy piece of paperback smut."

"Now I *am* worried," Bo said. "Should we call a shrink?"

"Call me crazy," Ardie said, "but I think your best bet is a priest. This kid believes in possession. Let's get the local witch doctor to cast the devils out."

Bo ran his thumb along the angle of his jaw. *This is the worst idea you've had yet,* said his little voice. Bo took out his phone and flipped it open. He punched in Gavin Gilroy's number and waited for the man to answer.

"Hi. Yeah, I know. Well, I don't care how busy you are. Tell Sir Rhys's flunky to blow him. That ought to keep them both busy. I need a favor." Bo was quiet for a few moments and then spoke again. "Point taken, I realize I'm not in charge. Now here's what I need. Can you get the vicar over here? Or would that be against policy?" Another silence from Bo, and then, "I appreciate it. As soon as you can wipe present company off your shoes, get Gryf to bring you down to the torture chamber." Bo listened and then replied. "No, we just call it that because that's where we party down with the whips and chains. Of course, it's a real torture chamber. Or was. Hey, Gavin? Thanks, man. I appreciate it."

"You're a real people person," Ardie remarked when Bo hung up.

"Fuck you, Ardie," Bo said cordially. "Shit, look at him. It's enough to make you believe in Spanish fly."

"His motor is definitely turning over," Ardie said. "Wonder who switched him on?"

Bo glanced at his watch without answering and Ardie looked curiously at his oldest friend.

"No comeback?" Ardie asked.

"Sorry, just a little worried."

"That's usually when you start bantering," Ardie said. "What's up?"

"I told you. The kid acted like that before. So hot for it he couldn't even talk."

"What about you?" Ardie said, taking Tristan's hot, dry hand in his.

"What?"

"You don't jump in the sack with just anybody," Ardie said. "You're not like that. So why did you do it? Why didn't you push him away?"

"I... couldn't."

"I'll believe anything you tell me and swear it's the truth under oath, but this is Twilight Zone material, you know?"

"You don't believe in ghosts any more than I do," Bo said. "If we did, we'd have to admit there's an afterlife."

"And change our evil ways," Ardie completed the litany. "This is very weird, though."

"I know."

"As long as we're in agreement," Ardie said. "Everything else will be cake."

Bo squeezed Ardie's shoulder, and the two men shared a smile. Suddenly Tristan's back arched, and the young man cried out sharply. Planting his feet against the floor, the young man lifted his pelvis as though meeting a lover halfway. Little mewling noises escaped his throat as his legs pumped, and he rocked as though taking some man's hard length into his sheath.

"Sweet Jesus!" The mild curse was loud in the silence.

Ardie and Bo turned as Morgan Idris slogged into the room, soaking wet.

"Where the hell did you come from?" Bo asked.

"Ah, merciful heavens, make it stop!" Morgan sobbed as he stared at Tristan, tears mixing with the salt water on his face. "Get it off the poor lad!"

"Hey, Morgan," Bo said with forced brightness. "How are you tonight? Why don't we go have a drink?"

"Let me help him," Morgan insisted. "I can make it go away."

"I have no idea what you're talking about," Bo said.

"Don't ya see it?" Morgan's eyes were still locked on Tristan.

The Irishman could clearly see the ghost ravishing the pretty lad on the floor of this terrible place. The apparition had the seeming of a well-built man with pale skin, eyes like onyx and dark hair that fell in waves to his shoulders. With wild abandon, the revenant thrust into its victim. Morgan fell to his knees weeping as the assault continued.

Sir Alun turned from his pleasant task and smiled at Morgan. "He's so full of life," the ghost said.

"Monster!" Morgan sobbed. "Why are you tormenting that poor lad?"

"We must feed," the apparition said, never missing a stroke. "The other hosts were... weak, but this youth bursts with energy, and he invited me."

Morgan had no doubt what the ghost meant by these words. "Cillian," the Irishman gasped, looking heavenward. "Forgive me! I didn't mean to harm you."

"What the devil's going on in here?" Gavin Gilroy asked as he entered.

"Constable," the vicar shouted from behind the policeman. "I insist you remove that drunk immediately."

Morgan looked around wildly as Ardie started toward him. Bo held his arms out as if herding a stray sheep, and Morgan swerved away from him.

"No," Morgan yelled. "Let me be. Let me help the poor lad."

"I think you've helped enough poor lads from what I just heard," Gavin said, grabbing Morgan's wrist. "You'd better come along with me and spend the night in the lockup. Tomorrow when you're sober, you'll be answering a few more questions for me."

Morgan flung himself away and crashed into Bo. Both men went down, and Bo held onto the Irishman as they fetched up against Ardie. Morgan wrenched around and stretched out his hand.

"Don't let that madman touch the boy," the vicar called out.

Ardie grabbed Morgan by the shoulders and rolled him away from Tristan. Gavin lunged and snapped a handcuff around Morgan's wrist. Hauling up on the steel bracelet, Gavin pulled Morgan farther away from the writhing victim.

"No," Morgan sobbed. "Let me touch him. I must touch him."

"Filthy pervert," the minister said. "I pray for you, Morgan Idris."

Morgan stared wild-eyed at the priest. "Help me, Father," the Irishman pleaded. "Tell them. I have the Sight. I can see the evil creature havin' its way with the lad. The glanconer will ravish him until it drains him."

"You poor soul," the vicar said. "Poor, deluded soul. Constable, I think it would be wisest if Mr. Idris underwent a psychiatric examination rather than being put with the more common criminals. For his own safety."

"That's a good idea," Gavin agreed. "Come along now," he said, pulling Morgan's arm.

"No!" Morgan screamed, frantically trying to pull away, calling on his goddess. "Brigid! Lady, help me do your bidding."

The Irishman succeeded in breaking Gavin's grip, but with his hands cuffed behind his back, he promptly fell on his face. With Bo's assistance, Gavin hauled Morgan to his feet and steadied him. Gavin dragged Morgan away, the Irishman cursing all the way down the hall and up the stone stairs. The vicar ignored the shouting and came to kneel beside Tristan and Ardie. As the priest reached for Tristan's hand, Sir Alun faded like an old Polaroid.

"Poor child," the minister said. "He suffers. Satan's hand lies heavy on him."

Ardie held his tongue out of respect for the uniform. Sean Carnes was a man of the cloth, and though Ardie was not a believer, he was not a scoffer, either. The vicar touched Tristan's cheek, and the liaison quieted.

"Do you think I might have a moment to pray with him?" Carnes asked.

"Sure," Ardie said, getting to his feet.

Ardie joined Bo, and they watched the vicar take one of Tristan's hands between his and bow his head. Without a word spoken, Ardie and Bo turned and gave the minister privacy.

"The kid seems to have settled down," Bo said.

"Yeah," Ardie said. "I know it was my idea, but I'm not sure now that a priest...."

"Ardie, some day you have to put the reservation behind you. Not all clergy are like the monks who taught at your school."

"I know. I probably just need some rest."

"We all do," Bo said. "Let's hope we get it."

"Gentlemen," the vicar said. "I think your young friend is feeling better now."

Bo and Ardie turned to see Tristan sitting up and looking around like a child who falls asleep at granny's house and wakes up in his own bed. The young man's eyes touched Ardie's, and then Bo's, before focusing on the vicar.

"I know you, don't I?" Tristan said.

"Like any pure soul, you respond to the power of my God within me," Carnes said.

Tristan frowned. "If you say so, Father," he said. "Thank you for waking me. I was having a very disturbing nightmare."

"My reward is in my service to my Lord," the vicar said. "But I accept your thanks. If you would care to talk about your nightmares, my door is always open."

"I'm absolutely done in," Tristan said. "If you'll excuse me, I think I need to lie down more than I need answers."

The vicar stood and offered his hand, but Tristan got to his feet on his own. Combing his disheveled hair with his fingers, Tristan started for the door. Bo caught the young man as his knees gave way. Putting the young man's arm around his neck, Bo encircled the slim waist and half-carried Tristan out of the dungeon. As they passed a gaping doorway on the next level, Tristan contrived to throw Bo off balance, and they fell into the room. Bo landed on his shoulder and rolled to a stop with Tristan atop him. Tristan's face was centimeters from Bo's, his eyes melting with lust. Bo's cock hardened as the young man ground against him.

"Tristan," he said reasonably, "I don't think this is a good idea."

"Why? Because I'm a nutcase?"

Taken aback by hearing his thoughts spoken aloud, Bo answered quickly. "No! Well, yeah, kind of. This is all a little crazy."

Tristan's stiff shaft rolled over Bo's. "Is this crazy?" he purred.

"Ahhh," Bo groaned. "Yes, it's insanity. Stop that."

"You mean this?" Tristan asked as he shifted his hips again.

"I said stop."

"I'm not deaf," Tristan made a subtle humping motion.

"Why are you doing this?"

"I'm hot and horny, and you're hung and hairy."

"Dirty talk," Bo said. "You're not fighting fair."

"I don't want to talk. I want to fuck. I want you to put your cock in me, thrust, and repeat until we both cum like geysers."

"Normally, there's nothing I'd like better, but I think you might be a little vulnerable right now. You should go to bed, by yourself, and we'll talk about this tomorrow."

"I want to fuck now," Tristan said petulantly.

"Well, I'm not playing along anymore," Bo said. "You caught me by surprise the first time, but it won't work again. I like sex as much as the next guy, but this is too weird."

The young man's eyelids drooped, and his lower lip protruded in a pout. "But I really want to."

"Stop," Bo said sternly as the lap dance resumed.

"Make me," Tristan taunted in a throaty voice as he mashed his cock against Bo's.

"Son of a bitch!" Bo cursed as the young man rocked against him.

Tristan laughed softly as he held Bo pinned and mimicked thrusting against him. Bo struggled to throw the young man off, but

Tristan was quite a bit stronger than he appeared. Bo's attempts to free himself only created greater friction.

"Fuck," Bo groaned as his eager cock twitched and disgorged sticky fluid inside his jeans.

Tristan got off the man and grabbed his own cock through the silky track pants. Rapidly, the young man fisted his hard length, eyes closed, white teeth embedded in his lower lip. Bo lay catching his breath, his heart racing as he watched the beautiful young man masturbate. What Tristan had just done to him was tantamount to rape, but it was one of the most powerful climaxes Bo had ever experienced. As he tried to sort out his feelings, a wink of gold on the fingers moving against soft navy fabric lulled Bo into a near-trance state.

He lay on the stones of the temple floor, his life running into the cracks in a red flood. With his dying sight, he watched the invader lift the avatar to the altar. In horror, he saw the unbeliever expose his manhood and ravish the Goddess's servant. The armored intruder wore a cross upon his back and took the virgin avatar like the cheapest whore. Tears blurred Bo's vision as he wept at his helplessness, racking sobs filling his ears. A cry of fulfillment jarred Bo out of his reverie, and he watched the fabric of Tristan's track pants darken with moisture. The tip of the liaison's tongue showed between his teeth as he sighed and released his sated shaft.

"What the hell just happened?" Bo asked, getting to his feet.

Tristan lips curved in an impish smile, but he didn't speak

Bo stared at the young man for a long moment. "Is this really how you want to play it?" he asked. "Because I don't care much for games."

"You are not required to enjoy it," Tristan said. "But you must play."

The young man walked away from Bo, leaving the salvager staring after him with an incredulous expression on his face. Bo had been with more than one young man his friends had termed "users," Chris being the most recent example. However, none of the previous poisonous beauties had possessed anything like Tristan's breathtakingly brutal honesty. Bo realized that nine out of ten men probably wouldn't understand his hesitation. They'd tell him to get some while the getting was good and get out before the heartaches started, but Bo had never been able to do that. He always hung on. Tristan had rocked Bo's world, making him do things against his better judgment. Bo didn't believe in ghosts, and he was leery of psychiatry, but there had to be some explanation for the way Tristan was behaving. He would rather believe he was possessed or crazy than that he just couldn't keep it in his pants. He got to his feet and dusted off his hands, no closer to understanding than before, but determined to get a grip on this situation. Until he did, there would be no more fooling around with gorgeous but seriously unhinged Tristan Lambert.

CHAPTER EIGHT

"I'M CALLING the institute," was the first thing Ardie said to Bo at their five a.m. meeting. "They said the kid might behave oddly, but I don't think this is what they meant. I admit, I don't understand exactly what it is he does, but I think this situation is too much for him."

"Good idea," Bo said. "Sir Rhys will be here soon for his official tour. I'm going to have a walk around and check on Gryf. Are you okay?"

"Have you known me not to be?" Ardie answered.

"Point taken. Don't hesitate to use the radio if you need me."

"Have I ever?"

"That's my boy," Bo smiled. "Nothing fazes you."

"That's what it says on the men's room wall," Ardie replied. "Go on now, pard. You're keeping me from working." Ardie pointedly took out his phone and began stabbing at the buttons.

"You know, it's okay that you're worried about the kid," Bo said softly. "I am too."

Ardie rolled his eyes and pointed to the phone.

Bo shook his head. "Tough guy," he muttered, but he was smiling fondly as he turned away and headed for the double staircase.

"MY LORD," Richard said, his voice as hollow as a bronze bell in the cavernous room.

"Aye, my lion?" Alun raised his head, surfacing from a narcotic memory of the harem he'd kept in the Holy Land.

"You are still too weak, my lord. You must feed again before you attempt this, but it seems as though some power favors this witch. Each time we begin the ravishment, something happens to prevent completion."

"Only from you will I accept a gainsaying of my will," Alun said, his eyes flashing. "I love you well, Richard; you are my right arm. But I will not hesitate to cut off that arm if it should betray me with disloyalty."

"I am loyal," Richard said. "I am not bound to you by spells like the Saracen or by greed like Odilon. I gave you my blood oath in life; I will not fail you even in death."

"I do not doubt you," Alun put a hand on Richard's shoulder. "And you are right. I must increase my strength before I can utterly consume the witch."

Aqil appeared in answer to Alun's silent summons. "What do you require of me, lord?"

"I need to feed again," Alun said. "That damned mortal intruded in a most untimely manner. Aqil, may I feed without calling my minion?"

The magus bowed his head, masses of ebony hair sliding forward on his shoulders. "Aye, lord. It is being arranged. Now that the witch wears your token, it will be easier to influence him from afar."

Bo WALKED the upper reaches of Caer Gwarchod, inspecting all the areas that Gryf had tagged as suspect. He examined the stone carefully for signs of stress fractures. They would be blasting in the dungeon very soon, and Bo would prefer it if the whole pile of rocks didn't come down on their heads.

Satisfied with his inspection, he walked out into the blowing day. The sun was bright, but the air was chilly up here on the battlements. The bruise-dark clouds were stacked so high, Bo knew they had to topple soon and drench the earth below. The ocean was riddled with divots, each wave crested with a cap of creamy foam. A great and nameless longing pierced Bo's heart, and he walked forward to stand in an embrasure. He stared out at the line where the sky collided with the water while the capricious wind crept under his clothes, running cold fingers over his skin.

"It's beautiful in an uncompromising sort of way, isn't it?"

Bo didn't turn at the sound of Tristan's voice. Somehow it didn't surprise him that the psychic had found him here. It was as though Bo had come here to wait for him. The moment hung suspended like the gulls soaring the cliff face. It had always been thus. The man was drawn to the sea, and the avatar was drawn to the man. That never changed.

What's this nonsense? Bo's conscience nagged. *Get hold of yourself.*

Bo tried to concentrate, but everything seemed to be receding at a rapid rate. The small, dry voice seemed to come from some unimaginable distance, out past Pluto. Then the young man spoke, and Bo heard nothing but that sweet voice. A soft hand was laid over Bo's where it rested on the stone. Bo turned his hand palm up and interlaced their fingers. He did it deftly and without thinking, like an action performed so many times the muscles have a memory of it. The cool, slim fingers fit perfectly with his callused, capable hand.

Yes, they were perfectly balanced: the earthly with the mystical, the warrior and the priest, the guardian and the treasure. Without the other, neither would need to exist, nor could. They were two halves of a perfect whole and the name of that wholeness was Love.

The man turned, not caring if they should be seen, and took the lithe body of his lover in his arms. Temple law said that the avatar must remain virgin, but there was much they could do to pleasure one another without penetration. Lust flared as bare skin slid against bare skin and mouths met in a warm, wet collision of lips and tongues.

"What do you see?" Tristan whispered into Bo's ear when the kiss ended.

"You, only you," the man said fervently, kissing his way down the long neck, pulling the odd tunic over the young man's head.

"And who am I?"

"You are...." Bo's fingers tightened around Tristan's biceps as he looked up to meet the young man's eyes. "You are desire," he said. "And your beauty outshines Her stars."

"What's my name?"

"You know it is forbidden to speak it. Why do you tease me?"

Tristan fought the compulsion to give in and let the enthralled treasure hunter make love to him again. The liaison recognized the ghost's inimical will at work, but that did nothing to quell the rush of heat that lit his loins. Though it would be easy to surrender to the spell, Tristan resisted. He didn't want to feed the revenant the sexual energy that would add to its strength. However, when he tried to shake off the compulsion, he found himself struggling against his own attraction to Andressen, magnified one hundredfold. No matter how Tristan struggled to raise his gift, it remained stubbornly quiescent. The power that normally flowed through him was dammed, and he had the maddeningly elusive notion that he should know why. Tristan had to admit that he could not get free of the ghost's sway, and unlike previous encounters, he was sharply aware of all that was happening. Thus far, he had taken everything in stride, assimilated it, and kept moving forward, but the dead Crusader was so powerful that Tristan found he was wishing that Garry were here.

"If wishes were horses, beggars would ride."

Tristan concentrated on the wry voice as Bo lavished caresses on him. "Help us," the liaison requested.

Bo ignored the conversation as he coaxed the young man with light touches and wet kisses.

"He looks to be enjoying himself."

"He's under an inimical influence," Tristan said. "Oh... oh, shit, oh, that's nice." The young man moaned as Bo nuzzled the hollow between his clavicles.

"'Inimical influence'? Is that a special gifted term for evil spirit?"

"I don't like to categorize spirits." Tristan's words ended on a gasp.

"How politically correct of you."

Bo licked the nipple he had just bitten as he kneaded Tristan's buttocks.

"You're supposed to look after him," Tristan said accusingly.

"Am I?"

Tristan groaned as a hand slipped under the drawstring waist of his pants and cupped a bare buttock. Rough fingers crept into the young man's cleft, massaging and probing.

"Are you going to help or not?" Tristan asked.

"I don't fancy being snuffed out like a firefly in a jar."

"You're afraid of the spirit that haunts this place?"

"You should be too."

"Why? He's very powerful, but in the end, he's just a ghost. I'll eventually get the upper hand," Tristan said bravely.

"A tiger is just a cat. You won't heed me, but I'll warn you anyway. You have something he wants very, very badly, and he will break you open to get at it," the voice warned.

"He won't break me with sex," Tristan said firmly. "I know my body's limits."

"I said you wouldn't heed me."

Tristan was having great difficulty ignoring what Bo was doing to him. Standing sideways, with a hand down the front and back of Tristan's pants, Bo fisted the young man's arousal and nudged delicately at his rear entry.

"Help us," Tristan tried again to link with the acerbic presence.

The liaison's gift touched nothing but the pervasive force of the revenant's will, like a miasma rising from a stagnant swamp, growing thicker by the second. Accepting that they were facing this alone, Tristan tried to talk to Bo again. Perhaps Tristan couldn't break the ghost's control just yet, but he could learn more about the adversary.

"Who are you?" Tristan asked softly as the man nuzzled his neck.

"I have the honor to be your beloved," the man murmured.

"Beloved," Tristan said as the man licked the rim of his ear.

"Aye?"

"Where are we?"

The man sighed. "I know we should not do this in Her sacred temple, but I do not believe that She truly disapproves. It is only the Elders that frown upon it."

"Whose temple is this?"

Bo chuckled, as the tip of his finger eased into Tristan and the young man gasped. "It is your temple, my love. At least it is when you wear the seeming of She Who Made Us."

Tristan's eyebrows went up as he searched his brain for ancient Eastern cults that worshipped a Mother Goddess who was served by transvestites. It was extremely difficult to think with Bo sucking his nipple and stroking his cock.

"And what are you to me?" Tristan panted as his balls tightened.

"I am sworn to protect you with my life," Bo said against the smooth skin of the young man's chest.

Tristan felt a chill that had nothing to do with the rapidly dropping temperature. The dark clouds had reached them, blocking out the sun. A spectral light filtered through the thunderheads, leaching color from the world and causing anything white to glow like an afterimage. Tristan felt the ghost's will come to bear, and lust took him over. Bo groaned as his arousal was grabbed and stroked through his cargo pants. Tristan's breath caught in his throat as his cock was pumped to a faster pace. Bo's finger sank deeper in the tender opening. With a choked-off cry, Tristan coated the man's fist, and in the dungeon far below, the revenant exulted at the influx of raw energy.

"And I thought I made a funny face when I cum," Chris said as he stepped from the tower doorway to the parapet.

Tristan jumped guiltily away from Bo and snatched his sweatshirt from the ground. Pulling the garment over his head, Tristan walked away without a word. The salvager blinked in the strong sunlight, feeling as though he'd just woken from a very pleasant dream to the clanging of an alarm. *Let Tristan go*, he thought. Why subject the kid to Chris's acid tongue? For the life of him, Bo couldn't remember how he and the psychic had gotten into such a compromising position again, but he wished like hell Chris hadn't seen it.

"What are you doing here?" Bo asked before his ex could speak again. With Chris, the best defense was a good offense.

"I go where my employer goes," Chris said coolly. "Don't change the subject. Who was that luscious dish of delish that scampered off, clutching at his pearls with such schoolgirlish mortification?"

"I'm not inclined to talk to you about him," Bo answered. "What are you doing here?"

"I... work... for... Sir... Rhys," Chris explained slowly.

"For how long?" Bo ignored the sarcasm.

"Immaterial."

"Bullshit! You're here to torture me. You got a taste for it and now you can't stop. You're an addict, Chris, and my pain is your drug of choice."

"You're so fucking arrogant," Chris said. "Of course this is about you. I've nothing else to do with my time but plan my revenge on a man that I dumped."

Bo's laugh was an ugly thing that contained no humor. "Dumped. You do have a way with words. You flushed me like a piece of shit. I don't think that rent-a-twink stopped sucking your dick for a second while you were tossing me out of the flat."

Chris rolled his eyes. "He was nothing. A piece of fluff that stuck to me when I left the club. That wasn't what you objected to and we both know it."

"You don't know shit," Bo said coldly. "You tried to break my heart, Chris, and you damn near did. I don't know why you're the way you are and, frankly, I no longer care. I just want you to take your show on the road."

"Yes, you looked quite brokenhearted when I walked out here," Chris said.

"I told you, don't talk about him."

"Oh please! Like he's too good for me to sully."

"That's right," Bo said. "You taint everything you touch."

"Oh, Bo," Chris said archly. "Where's your sense of drama? Why have a boring old love affair with a ruggedly gorgeous guy when you can make a play for his equally gorgeous best friend and drive a wedge between them? I love soap operas, don't you?"

"What did I ever find attractive about you?" Bo wondered aloud.

"If memory serves, it was my arse," Chris said. "I was wearing very tight, very white pants with no knickers. You fucked me against the wall of the glass elevator in that sexily expensive hotel at four in the morning."

"You had lube and condoms in your pocket."

94

Chris shrugged. "You thought it was cute."

"I was hammered."

"You still got it up for me."

"I'll never win a battle of words with you, Chris," Bo said. "Convince your tame nobleman to take you home. Tell him you're having Harrods withdrawal pains or something."

"We're not leaving until you find that treasure, my well-hung friend," Chris said, all the honey extracted from his voice. "Sir Rhys the Colossal Cunt wouldn't have come near this place if not for me. He'd prefer to forget it exists."

"Okay, now I know your agenda. You're fucking for profit rather than entertainment this time. Now get the fuck out of here. I'll mail you his lordship's share."

Chris smiled winsomely, but his voice was cold as a razor against someone's throat. "When did you grow the balls to think you could give orders to me? I'm a counter-puncher, Bo. You know that. I'll take whatever you throw at me and throw it back harder."

"I won't trade hits with you," Bo said. "I'll turn Ardie loose on your ass. He's aching for a chance at a rematch."

Something akin to fear flickered in Chris's pale green eyes. "We'll be staying in rooms above the pub in Drws," he said. "We won't be here at the castle all the time."

"I'm not being clear," Bo said. "Stay the fuck away from me and everyone associated with me. If you don't, I'll acquaint Sir Rhys with some of your less reputable history."

"He won't care."

"Right," Bo said. "I've forgotten just how good you are at sucking cock."

Chris leaned closer to Bo and smiled. "Best head you'll ever get," he said.

Turning on his heel, Chris walked away, leaving a scowling Bo in his wake. Descending the winding stairs of the tower, he tried to erase the vision of Bo pressing that beautiful lad to the wall. Who *was* this annoyingly stunning young man who excited Bo enough to snog outdoors in broad daylight where anyone, including ex-boyfriends, might see them? Chris couldn't imagine anything more erotic than having it off in front of other people, and had begged Bo to make love in public on many occasions, only to be rebuffed. It was a kink that Sir Rhys was more than willing to indulge, but Chris chafed in the role of submissive subordinate. He liked being the one to crack the whip, so to speak, as Bo had allowed him to do for a while. Chris had known he would have trouble with the man eventually. Bo was indulgent in the bedroom, but out of it, he couldn't be backed down by an inch. However, Chris wouldn't have come here if he didn't think he could handle Bo. Chris knew all of Bo's soft spots, thanks to the man's habit of speaking honestly and openly to his lovers.

Chris reached the second landing and left the staircase. As he stepped into the hall, he had the feeling that this was the wrong floor and turned to go back to the stairs. His eyes widened and he stopped in his tracks.

"You are very fair," Sir Alun said, glowing faintly with the energy given off by Tristan's orgasm. "Let me fulfill your fantasies."

"Fuck off, you role-playing geek," Chris said.

Chris walked purposefully toward the big man in the medieval costume. The fellow was handsome and reeked of virility, but he probably lived with his mum.

Sir Alun moved into Chris's path.

"Don't make me tear you a new one, mate," Chris said.

Sir Alun smiled.

Chapter Nine

THE sound of a harsh gasp was loud in the empty tunnel.

"Ahhh, I love it when you've just trimmed your nails and oh...." James's words trailed off in a long groan.

Gryf took his lover's hard length down his throat again, running his fingernails over the insides of the Scot's thighs. James's knees trembled as he sagged back against the twelfth-century wall they were about to blow a hole in, literally as well as figuratively.

"Ah, Gryf, you make me so hard I could take down this wall without the bloody explosives," James groaned, glancing over at the package attached to the wall. Those were his last coherent words for a few moments as his lover did all the things he loved at the same time.

As soon as Gryf swallowed, he got to his feet and went to inspect their work for the last time. "James love, put your willie away and have a look at the remote charges before you go back to the Big Ass Book. And don't pout or I won't shag you later."

"You're cruel and inhuman," James said, as he zipped up.

"That's why we get along so well," Gryf said unconcernedly. "Go on. We'll take up right where we left off, as soon as we're off the clock. Then you can get me off, so to speak."

James looked at his watch. "Let's stop wasting time with bad puns then," he said and started down the tunnel with his flashlight.

"James," Gryf called, and his lover turned around with a scowl. "I love you."

A smile bloomed across James's boyish face. Blowing Gryf a kiss, he walked off.

"Cheeky bugger," Gryf said fondly. "Prepare for the big bang, because that's what I'm going to give you tonight." With pleasant thoughts of James stripped naked and riding him like a Derby winner, Gryf looked down at the connections he was checking.

CHRIS stood his ground, as he had ever done, as the big, handsome devil advanced on him. Chris had much experience of big, handsome devils and didn't doubt that he could handle this one in the same fashion. Tilting his face up, Chris gave the stranger an opportunity to be impressed by his looks.

"Do you have permission to go wandering around up here?" Chris asked.

"Why should I need anyone's leave to walk here?" Alun asked in surprise at the young man's tone of authority.

"It's really not safe," Chris said. "The treasure hunters are…."

"The treasure is mine," Alun interrupted fiercely.

Chris took another look at the stranger in the extremely authentic-looking costume. Was it possible that Chris had run across the local crackpot? Crackpots were not usually so well groomed. This robust fellow wasn't wild-eyed or disheveled. In fact, the odd stranger was the very picture of a medieval lord of the manor in fur-trimmed velvet.

"I think you'd better tell me your name," Chris said, giving the interloper his patented cold, superior face.

Alun smiled in a quicksilver change of mood. "My name, fair one? I will give you that and much more besides. What will you give me?"

Chris paused again before answering; the stranger hadn't responded in a way that Chris had predicted, and he had no ready reply. In the silence, Alun moved closer.

"Neither the salvagers, the police, nor the owner will take it kindly if they find you here," Chris blurted out.

"The owner?" Alun's smile grew wider. "I think he will not mind."

"Is that right?" Chris gave the nutcase a preview of what his real sneer was like. "Well, as it happens, I know the owner, and I can tell you unequivocally that he would mind very much."

"How well do you know him, fair one?" Alun asked, leaning toward Chris.

For the first time since puberty, Chris became flustered. "I... I work for him," he stammered.

"Are you a liege man or a serf?" Alun said in a voice so freighted with innuendo that Chris knew his answer was important.

"Well, I'm certainly not a serf," Chris answered. "That's like a peasant, right? I'm his lordship's secretary."

"And I am certain you know well how to wield a pen, but tell me: who is this imposter who calls himself lord of this land?"

Chris felt that odd frisson of wrongness again. The intruder in the wine-dark tabard didn't seem like someone playing dress up. The stranger wore the clothing as if he put it on every morning. There was a worn look to the rich fabrics that stage costumes didn't have. And there was something teasingly familiar about the design stitched large in gold across the breast of the long surcoat.

"It's a manticore," Chris said abruptly. "You have a manticore on your tabard, like the one on Sir Rhys's crest." He stopped speaking as suddenly as he had started. His eyes widened as they traveled up from the stranger's broad chest to the handsome face. "Oh my God!"

"BO!" ARDIE called out as he caught sight of the man.

Bo met his partner at the bottom of the sweeping double staircase. "What is it? I want to check with Gryf before the blast."

"Have you seen Chris? Sir Rhys's ready for a nap or a diaper change… or maybe he just needs something to suck on," Ardie said.

"Or somebody to suck on him," Bo took the straight line Ardie handed him. "I just had a run-in with the spawn of Satan up on the battlements."

Ardie cringed comically, and then pretended to check Bo's neck for puncture wounds. "So what did the Prince of Darkness want?" he asked.

"I don't know if he was looking for me or not," Bo said. "But when he ran into me, we had a little boundary-setting session."

"Right on," Ardie said. "He was probably up there trying to avoid me or his boss."

"Sorry you have to deal with Turcotte, Ardie," Bo said. "But you know him better than we do. And here's another sin we can lay at Chris's feet. He talked Turcotte into coming here."

"Bitch!" Ardie exclaimed.

Lord Turcotte entered the hall behind Ardie and Bo. "I believe it's the first time I've ever been called a bitch," Rhys said.

Ardie made a face. "I wasn't talking about you," he said. "I was referring to Chris."

"Oh," Lord Turcotte said. "Yes. I had noticed that tendency in him, but he doesn't indulge it with me. I find, gentlemen, that a quick and severe taste of discipline at the first sign of temper will usually discourage repeat performances."

Ardie and Bo exchanged an incredulous glance. "Sounds like you know how to handle your employees," Bo drawled, winking at Ardie.

"Not so different from your style," Ardie one-upped his friend. "Maybe you and Sir Rhys can compare whips sometime."

Lord Turcotte looked from one man to the other. "That was sexual innuendo, wasn't it?"

"I must be losing my touch if you didn't recognize it," Ardie said.

"If you'll excuse me," Bo said. "I need to get downstairs."

"What's it like now... down there?" Rhys asked.

Something in the lord's tone made Bo take the time to answer him. "We've got lights in the lower levels," he said. "They push the dark back some, but you can see the shadows just waiting to reclaim everything when the generators are switched off. Tell you the truth: we don't turn 'em off. They're power efficient, so why not let 'em stay on?"

"Yes, I think that's probably a good idea," Rhys said. "In the dark, anything could happen."

Bo didn't think that Lord Turcotte was speaking of liability or lawsuits, but he didn't know the man well enough to follow up the remark.

"Besides the dark," Bo said, "there's the moisture and that dank smell. Part wet rock and earth and mold and something else I don't have a name for, worms maybe."

"Worms," Rhys repeated in a faraway voice. "Yes, something that crawls in the dirt and feeds on flesh."

Bo looked over at Ardie as Sir Rhys continued to speak.

"Big, fat, white worms that come out in the dark and...."

A thunderous boom followed by a concussive wave of air from the dungeon stairwell interrupted Lord Turcotte. Oblivious of the danger, Bo turned and ran for the stairs with Ardie right behind him. After a momentary hesitation, Sir Rhys followed them.

CHRIS flinched when he heard the blast and felt the vibration. The stranger took no notice whatsoever of the disturbance.

"You remind me of someone," Chris said, nonchalantly ignoring the explosion as well. "In Sir Rhys's home in London, there's a portrait of his ancestor, Sir Alun. It's not a particularly good painting, but I can see a likeness."

"I *am* Sir Alun," the ghost said.

Chris nodded. Lunatic, time traveler, or poltergeist, Chris didn't need to know which one the soi-disant Sir Alun was in order to manipulate him. Alun was an alpha male, and that's all the information Chris required.

"My lord," Chris said, lowering his eyelids, "you know of the intruders in your fortress?"

Alun smiled.

"They're looking for your treasure," Chris said.

Alun raised an eyebrow.

"I'll bet no one knows where it is but you, am I right?" Chris returned the ghost's smile.

Alun nodded, and Chris moved closer to the phantom.

"They want to take what's yours," Chris said, looking up into Alun's eyes. "I could help you stop them."

Alun cocked his head, looming over the slender man. "You would take my part in this? What of your master?"

"You are the true lord of Caer Gwarchod," Chris said. "The usurper is a weak man."

"You feel no loyalty to him?"

Chris spoke carefully, warned again by Alun's attitude that the answer was important. "I didn't take any oaths. He pays me a salary to do his bidding."

"You would do my bidding?"

"Yes, my lord."

"Why? And do not tell me it is because I am the rightful lord. I will not believe you."

Chris favored Alun with his charming sheepish expression. "I assume my lord would reward me," he said.

"Swear to serve me," Alun said, drawing himself up to his full height.

Chris took a deep breath, reminded himself of what he stood to gain, and said the words. "I swear I will serve you," he said.

Chris's expression of resolve didn't waver as Alun reached out to place a hand on his head. As fast as thought, Alun's other hand flew forward to pierce Chris's chest, sinking into the flesh to the wrist. Chris's face twisted in agony as an acute, galvanizing wire of pain froze a path from his heart down his left arm and back to his heart. It was over in a moment. Alun withdrew his hand, and warmth rushed back into Chris's limbs in a burning, prickling tide of sensation. The young man looked up at his new meal ticket with profound respect dawning in his eyes. This Alun was the real deal—more than a man, a powerful creature with unknown power.

"Tell me what you want," Chris invited in a soft voice.

"The witch must be mine," Alun said.

"Witch?" Chris repeated in utter surprise.

Alun's chilly fingers curled around Chris's long neck in a gesture at once tender and threatening. "You know him," he said. "You spoke with him on the bastions. A youth with the sort of beauty that doomed Troy."

"Bo's revenge fuck?" Chris exclaimed. "A witch? Ah, of course, he's the psychic. I understand whom your lordship means."

"What do you know of him?"

Chris smiled up at Alun. "The witch's name is Tristan," Chris said. "He speaks to spirits, I understand. And evicts them from their homes."

"I will drink his soul like warm milk," Alun said fiercely. "And fill his sweet flesh with my essence, and he will give me life everlasting."

Chris blinked, assimilating this madness before he replied. "I will do what I can to help you, my lord," he said. "What is... your bidding?"

"My minion has placed upon the boy a token that is bound to my essence," Alun said. "Through it, I may influence him and feed from his energy, but he has become wary, and I cannot bring him to me. You must do this."

"How?"

"When the time is propitious, you will know," Alun assured Chris. "Now there is another service you may do me."

"My lord?"

"I hunger," Alun said.

Chris didn't pretend to misunderstand. "Here, my lord?"

Alun's sinister smile reappeared. "Wherever you like, fair one. Open your thoughts to me," the revenant answered.

Chris gasped as the dark walls wavered, melted, and became brocade curtains of cream and gold. He floated rather than fell to his back on a mattress like a cloud covered in vanilla velvet. Rose petals—pink, yellow, and white—drifted through air heavy with ancient perfumes. The softly glowing lamps were ivory and gold, no less beautiful than Chris's naked flesh.

"It's gorgeous," Chris breathed, looking at the big man lying beside him on the bed.

"It is your domain, whenever you wish to visit," Alun said.

Chris boldly placed a hand on the revenant's arousal. "You are generous, my lord," he said with a leer.

"And you are very fair," Alun said as Chris's mouth covered the head of his shaft.

In this half-world between waking and unconsciousness, Sir Alun was as solid as he wished to be. He was quite solid just now and hard as the stone of his castle, as Chris could attest. The young man blocked out everything but the thought of the treasure and let his well-trained body do what it did best as the ghost lay indolently back against the pillows. As Chris straddled the revenant and lowered himself onto the long shaft, Sir Alun moved at last. His large hands went around Chris's waist, helping to support the young man. Chris looked down with the beginning of a smile when Alun's grip tightened. Holding Chris's eyes, Alun forced him down onto the hard length until it was sheathed.

Chris's conflicting emotions were a banquet of diverse flavors that Alun sampled at his leisure. The lord ran his hands across the young man's lightly furred chest, down the trembling inner thighs, to the drooping stalk of Chris's manhood. At the revenant's touch, Chris's cock quivered and rose like a trick of time-lapse photography. Chris's pretty mouth fell open, and he drew in a great breath. Before he could release it in a cry of mingled pain and pleasure, the ghost put a finger to his lips. Chris nodded, biting at his lower lip as the thick shaft moved in his passage. Bracing himself on hands and knees, crouched over his new master, Chris began to rock, impaling himself to the rhythm of music only he could hear.

As his new minion writhed with seeming bliss on his staff, Alun tested his control. An intense orgasm bloomed in Chris's groin, and he swallowed his cry of pleasure as he bore down on the shaft that stretched him. Alun rose from the mattress to float above it, and Chris clutched at the revenant's shoulders as they levitated into an upright position. Alun cupped the young man's buttocks, and Chris quickly wrapped his legs around the phantom. Bearing Chris's weight as if the young man were inflatable, Alun thrust up into the wet heat that hugged his length so tightly. Intoxicated by Chris's fluids and endorphins, the ghost exerted his will to keep his minion aroused. To his delight, Chris was much more susceptible and responsive than Sean.

Chris's head swam with the sensory overload his system was experiencing. He'd never had the nerve to take hallucinogenic drugs and was reasonably sure this was not a flashback. He had to accept that he was floating somewhere near head-height, being thoroughly ravished by the spirit of a Crusader knight. The world changed for Chris in that moment; it seemed to pause in its rotation, tilt slightly, and then begin spinning at a faster pace. Reality fell out from under him in the same way the bed had. He was adrift in space, and the revenant was a black hole that was slowly but inexorably drawing him in. Chris groaned as he came again, and his seed evaporated as it left his body. Before his cock could begin to soften, Chris felt another climax building in his groin.

"You have much more to give, fair one," Alun murmured in Chris's ear. "Hold on to me."

Chris did as he was told, lacing his fingers behind Alun's neck and hooking his ankles behind the ghost's thighs. Alun's head tilted, and his body followed suit until he hovered face down with Chris clinging to him. Digging his fingers into Chris's ass, Alun thrust hard and fast into the snug socket until Chris came again, clenching his jaw to hold in a wail of pleasure. He could do this. He could take whatever this spook dished out. *I ain't afraid a no ghost*, he thought, smothering a giggle.

Alun looked into his minion's eyes, saw the seeds of madness take root, and knew that this one would break quickly. It mattered little, and he returned his attention to extracting as much energy as possible from his victim.

"NO, PLEASE God, no," Bo Andressen uttered the desperate little prayer over and over without realizing it as he ran toward the blast site.

Ardie stopped behind Bo and stared at the destruction. Dust hung in the air over the rubble of stone blocks that had stood there since the twelfth century. The east tunnel no longer existed; it was completely filled in. The target wall had collapsed as planned, but so had the passageway. It shouldn't have been possible, but they were staring at the indisputable evidence.

Ardie pulled out his cell phone. "I need to speak to Officer Gilroy," he said. "I don't care what he's doing; interrupt him. Tell him… tell him there may have been more deaths at the castle, and don't tell anyone else."

Rhys arrived as Bo and Ardie began inspecting the wreckage. Ardie knew this was going to be harder on Bo than anyone else, the same way he knew that a search would find no one alive in the debris. Some things were self-evident. Resignedly, Ardie intercepted Lord Turcotte before the man could accost Bo and steered the nobleman back into the hall.

Chapter Ten

"YOU see them, don't you?" the vicar encouraged Morgan.

The pale green walls of the hospital room were closing in on Morgan Idris. He tried not to look at Sean Carnes, for fear the young clergyman could see all his sins. The narcotics that swam in the Irishman's bloodstream made time as inconsequential as water dripping from a tap. They also made him extremely biddable.

"Try and focus on me, Morgan," the vicar said. "I don't want to administer more drugs, but I will if I must."

Brigid, Morgan called silently. *Help me, Lady.*

Carnes's smooth brow creased slightly. "I'm here to help you," he said. "But you must trust me. Be truthful, Morgan. You see them, don't you?"

"Who?" Morgan finally spoke.

"The things that go bump in the night, of course," the vicar said. "The ghosts. You see them. I know you do."

"That's mad," Morgan said slowly. "No such thing as ghosts."

"Is there anything more obstinate than an Irishman?" the minister muttered. "Morgan, you must know that terrible things are happening at Caer Gwarchod. Don't you want to help?"

"I want a drink," Morgan said.

"I'm afraid that wouldn't be a good idea right now," Carnes said. "I have a doctorate in psychiatry as well as divinity, but I need neither one to know that narcotics and alcohol are a killer combination. Why don't you just talk to me? We'll have a nice chat, and then you can have a rest with some more of those very nice drugs."

Something sparked in Morgan's dull gaze. "You wouldn't put me away, would you?" he said. "I've told you I don't believe in ghosts, and I don't see 'em either. Don't send me to the loony bin, Vicar. I don't like it there."

"You're not leaving us much choice," Carnes said. "Public drunkenness, vagrancy, supplying liquor to minors.... I could go on, but I think you know your sins better than I. The police want to lock you up, Morgan. I'm suggesting you be sent to a facility where you can receive care instead of abuse."

"What do you want me to say?" Morgan asked. "Just tell me. Only don't send me back there, please."

"You see them, don't you?" the vicar asked again.

"Aye," Morgan answered wearily. "I see the ghosts. And I see the guardian spirits. Of people. Of animals. Of bloody trees. They're all around us. The fuckin' air is thick with 'em. I've always seen 'em. Used to drive me Ma mad when I'd go on about the pretty folk. She'd take a strap to me, but it did no good. I still see 'em."

"And that's why you drink so much," the clergyman said.

"I have to do something to drown them out," Morgan sighed. "If I lived in London, maybe I'd be on smack. Who bloody knows?"

"It's all right, Morgan," Carnes reached across the space that separated them and touched Idris's shaggy hair. "I'm going to take care of you."

"You don't believe me, either," Morgan said. "You're going to let them drug me and strap me down and run electricity through me like a bloody toaster. Please, Vicar, help me."

Carnes stood and Morgan looked up at him. The vicar smoothed the tangled hair back from the Irishman's fearful face with a look of compassion. "Poor thing," the minister said soothingly. "The Sight's not an easy gift to bear, but you have my promise that you will have peace."

"Thank you," Morgan said, his eyes filling with tears. "Saint Brigid, forgive me."

"You pray to Brigid?" the vicar said. "Did you know that she was a pagan heroine who was adopted into the church centuries after her death? It was easier to just absorb her than to try and stamp out her worship in ancient Ireland. A tenacious goddess."

"I dream about her sometimes," Morgan said. "I like those dreams. In them, I'm a hero with a harp and a spear, and I do the Lady's bidding, fighting injustice and protecting the weak from harm."

"That's a lovely dream," Carnes said. "Are you on a mission right now?"

"I'm so tired," Morgan said. "Do we have to talk now?"

"I'm afraid so. I'm sorry, just a few more questions so I can help you with the police, and I'll let you sleep. Are you protecting someone now?"

"The one at the castle," Morgan said, beginning to slur his words. "He's like me."

"Are you speaking of the psychic?"

Morgan frowned. "Poor thing, they're all around him, the ghosties and hobgoblins. He's like a sun, and they're the flowers, you see? No, wait, he's a blossom, and they're bees."

The vicar nodded. "I understand the concept. Tristan radiates something that the spirits find attractive. Have I got it?"

Morgan slumped in his chair, his eyelids at half-mast. "They feed," he mumbled.

"Who feeds, Morgan?"

"The Lord of Caer Gwarchod."

"Sir Rhys!"

Morgan shook his head groggily. "No, the first one."

"You're not making sense," Carnes said. "Tell me, Morgan; did Saint Brigid give you a weapon to defeat this evil spirit?"

"She told me a secret." Morgan smiled dreamily.

"Would you like to confess it to me?"

"I'd like a drink," Morgan mumbled.

"It's all right if you tell me," the vicar said. "I'm a holy man. Please, Morgan, if you know anything at all helpful, tell me."

"Dagger," Morgan whispered as his eyes closed.

"Morgan?"

"Aye, Vicar?" the Irishman responded slowly.

"Tell me about the dagger."

A short time later, the vicar walked out of the regional medical facility. He smiled pleasantly at the charge nurse, the security guard, and the constable who was playing chauffeur at Gavin Gilroy's behest. However, beneath the pale, smooth-as-cream features and clear blue eyes, the vicar was anything but tranquil. In fact, he was terrified.

As the police car pulled away, a taxi took its place under the hospital's covered drive, and Sean Dymock got out. After a brief conversation with the nurse, who knew the publican well, Morgan's friend was allowed a brief visit.

"GOD save us," Gavin Gilroy said wearily as he dropped into a chair in the castle's main hall.

The group waiting silently around the coffee urn eyed the policeman with expressions ranging from apprehensive to impatient. Gavin looked up and thanked Ardie when the man handed him a cup of black coffee. Lord Turcotte cleared his throat and took it on himself to speak for everyone.

"Are you going to tell us what happened?" Rhys asked.

"Aye, Sir Rhys," Gavin said. "It's your castle; you've a right to know. I assume you don't mind if these gentlemen listen?"

Rhys swept his eyes over Ardie, Bo, Tristan, and lastly, Chris. The peer's eyes paused for a moment on his secretary, who'd gone missing all morning. Chris stared blandly back, and Rhys turned his attention to Gavin.

"I'm sorry," the policeman said, looking at the other men. "Remains of your team members have been found. There's no need for anyone to make identification. We'll do that with blood and tissue samples. I... I'm sorry."

"Can we see them?" Ardie asked.

Gavin closed his eyes briefly. "I wouldn't advise it," he said. "Remember your friends as they were. We'll be taking them out soon. That area is cordoned off now. No one goes down there. Am I understood?"

"You're letting us stay?" Bo asked.

"This appears to be an accident," Gavin said. "A terrible accident, but unintentional nonetheless. You can stay."

"Thanks," Bo said to Gavin.

Gavin nodded and rose, setting his cup on the table. "I'll be accompanying the bodies," he said. "Don't worry. I'll take care of them."

Gavin stood and held out his hand. Numbed, Bo didn't react for a moment. When the policeman took the salvager's hand, the warmth of the simple human contact undid Bo. His face crumpled along fault lines of sorrow, and tears overflowed as he turned away. His own eyes brimming, Ardie pulled Bo into an embrace. Bo hugged his best friend briefly, but fiercely, before letting him go. A moment later, they heard the forensics team enter the hall. The uniformed men walked solemnly to the front entrance carrying various bags and cases, none of them large enough to contain a human body. No one at the table wanted to dwell on the fact that Gryf and James hadn't merely been killed; they had been obliterated under tons of rock.

Gavin turned back before he reached the big doors. "Mind the storm," he said. "It's going to be a nasty one."

"We saw it building, and we're prepared," Bo assured him. "This castle has stood here for over nine hundred years. I think it'll make it through the storm."

"This is killing him," Ardie moved to Bo's side as he watched the policeman depart.

"Gilroy's a good man," Bo said. "He's tough. He'll weather this shit the same way Caer Gwarchod will weather the storm."

"And you?"

Bo turned to meet Ardie's eyes. "I'm numb. I can't fucking believe this happened. *How* could it happen? Gryf was one of the ten best explosives experts in the world. He was so anal that if you fed him a lump of coal, he'd shit a diamond."

"I know that, Bo," Ardie said softly.

"He loved James," Bo went on. "Gryf loved that kid, and he would never, ever in a million years do or not do anything that would cause Jamie harm. It couldn't happen."

"I know that too."

"Then what the fuck happened?" Bo demanded loudly.

Tristan looked up at the sound of the raised voice and saw Ardie put his arms around Bo. For a second, the young man experienced a curious doubling of the image he saw. Bo and Ardie stood about thirty feet away in a stray shaft of weak sunlight, leaning on one another's shoulders, weeping for their lost comrades. However, Tristan saw them in another guise. As he watched the grieving men, another tableau was superimposed over what he was seeing.

Bo's sun-bleached hair hung in two long braids, framing a face with a lot more scars. A sword and an ax hung from the gilded leather that belted his thigh-length tunic of undyed linen. The cuirass of overlapping bronze scales and elaborately tooled boots declared his status as an upper echelon warrior, captain of those hired to defend this temple. Next to him stood the high priest, his black tresses ornamented with gold, pearls, and rubies, his clothing naught more than a loincloth of the same linen as the warrior's tunic. Swirling arabesques of henna followed the contours of his sculpted face and flowed down his neck to spread across his pectorals. Viewed from a distance, the fluid design was clearly a tree in full flower with long, branching roots anchoring it to the earth.

Tristan knew in his bones that once before he had sat, as he was sitting now, hearing some dire news, watching his two most trusted counselors argue and then comfort one another. He did not doubt the veracity of the vision for a moment. He was not hallucinating; he was remembering something that had happened to him in another life. Slowly, so as not to attract attention, Tristan rose and left the hall.

Chris listened absently to Sir Rhys as he watched the young man walk away. Noticing his aide's inattention, Lord Turcotte gripped the other man's shoulder with a large hand.

"What's going on behind those big, pretty eyes, hmm?" Rhys asked.

"Nothing at all, sir," Chris said smoothly. "Except how I'm going to comply with your wish to be out of this cunting castle, off this bloody island, and the fuck out of Wales as quickly as possible. I've paged the driver. I'm sure he'll answer at any moment." Chris touched the phone in his pocket that hadn't been used in hours. There was no way Chris was going to leave the castle now, and that meant Sir Rhys would be staying as well. If the chauffeur were blamed for it, Chris wouldn't cry.

Rhys held his secretary's gaze for a long moment before releasing him. "Who is he?" the nobleman said.

"He?" Chris prompted.

"The man you're fucking. Which one is it? Gilroy? Red Dog? Andressen? Ah, I seem to have struck a nerve at last. And I wasn't sure you had any nerves." Sir Rhys raised an eyebrow. "So you're fucking the boss treasure hunter. I needn't wonder why, I suppose. Strictly a mercantile arrangement? Or do you fancy him?"

Chris got himself under control and answered blandly. "I've no idea what your lordship is talking about. It's true I knew Bo in the past, but I'm not sleeping with anyone but the lord of this castle. And I'm not sure you can refer to it as fucking, but I'm no expert."

"Aren't you?"

"May I go about my duties now?" Chris replied.

"One more question," Rhys said as he leaned closer to Chris. "Do you think the blast might have driven the monsters out of the dungeon?"

Chris remembered the terrible pleasures he had received at the hands of the phantom, and a shiver ran down his spine. "I'm sure it did, my lord," he said. "Can I get you some tea or coffee before I start making calls?"

"No, I need to talk to Andressen about the future of this project," Rhys said, glancing over at Bo and Ardie.

"Give him a few minutes, and remember what we have to gain by continuing the operation, sir," Chris said.

"I'll keep it in mind," Rhys said. "Somehow the tragic deaths of two men keep pushing aside the thought of treasure."

"There have been more than two," Chris pointed out softly as he turned away. Pulling his cell from his suit jacket, Chris strolled off in the direction Tristan had taken.

Sir Rhys glared at the young man's back; he was going to keep Chris on his knees for a long time tonight.

TRISTAN rose from the stone step as he heard footfalls. Dragging a sleeve across his eyes, he faced the intruder.

"Oh… hi," Chris said with a creditable counterfeit of surprise. "Sorry if I'm…."

"No," Tristan interrupted. "I'm just… It's all a bit much, you know?"

Chris nodded. "Tragic," he said. "If you want to be alone, I certainly understand."

"Wait," Tristan said. "I'm fine. I just had to have a cry where none of the other boys could see. I haven't spoken much to you."

"His lordship keeps me busy," Chris said.

"He seems like a difficult man to work for," Tristan said.

Chris grinned. "He's a proper bastard," he said. "But I don't plan to make a career of it."

"Do you live in London?" Tristan asked with interest.

"Why don't we take a walk?" Chris suggested. "And I'll tell you anything you want to know about babysitting a peer."

Tristan smiled tentatively. "All right," he said as he followed Chris upward.

"I WILL not let Gryf and James's deaths be for nothing," Bo told Lord Turcotte.

"If I withdraw my consent, you'll have no choice but to leave," Rhys said.

"Um, that's not quite true, sir," Ardie said. "We have a contract. That contract allows you to visit the job site as a consultant, but nowhere does it give you permission to exclude us. I'd hate to bring lawyers into this. You know how those sharks are; all they're interested in is their cut. They'll drag this out as long as possible to keep the fees coming in."

"Aren't you a lawyer, Mr. Red Dog?" Rhys asked.

"Yes, I am," Ardie said. "And you're making my point for me."

One of the big front doors banged open, forestalling Rhys's reply. They looked up from The Book as a cold draft of wet wind bullied its way into the hall. Gavin Gilroy, soaking wet in an oilskin slicker, pulled another man in from the driving rain and struggled to shut the door. Bo ran over to help as Gavin's companion sagged against the wall.

"Thanks," Gavin said as the door locked into place.

Bo nodded. "Back so soon?" he asked.

"Found this fellow wandering around the station and brought him over," the policeman said. "We won't be going back across until this squall blows itself out. Got a spare bunk?"

Why don't you ask him to share yours? asked the little voice in Bo's head.

"We'll find room for you," Bo said as Ardie stopped beside him.

"Dr. Arvel," Ardie said in surprise. "What are you doing here?"

"I discussed your call with Dr. Davies, and she agreed that I should be here," Garry said as he pulled back the hood of his raincoat. "It's possible you're dealing with a very nasty breed of ghost."

"Can't say I'm sorry you're here," Ardie said. "Though, given a choice, I would have chosen Dr. Davies."

"Welcome to the club," Garry said wryly. "Now, tell me in detail what you told Alicia on the phone."

CHAPTER ELEVEN

GARRY hung the now-damp towel on the back of the chair and gratefully accepted the steaming cup that Bo held out.

"Thank you," Garry said. "I'm chilled to the bone."

"I'm sorry you had to come out in this weather," Ardie said. "I wasn't really expecting you. I thought you'd give me a call back with some information or something."

"You've no idea what you're dealing with, do you?" Garry said.

"Why don't you tell us?" Bo suggested.

"Mr. Andressen," Garry said. "From what Mr. Red Dog told me on the phone, you've got a revenant here."

"And just what sort of thing is that?" Lord Turcotte asked.

"Give them the short course you gave me at the station," Gavin advised Garry.

Garry nodded. "Ghosts are drawn by human emotions and can absorb the resonance of very strong ones, such as fits of rage or acts of love. The vibrations of powerful feelings are like fuel or food to them. Given enough raw emotion to feed on, incorporeal spirits can become capable of physical acts such as knocking sounds, cold spots, slamming doors, and the sort of incidents one associates with the term 'poltergeist'. But what you have here is nothing as innocuous as a poltergeist."

Garry paused, but his audience didn't seem disposed to interrupt with questions.

"Revenants are rather more serious than your generic house-haunter. They consume human essences to keep them anchored to this plane and give them strength. They cannot suck blood from the veins, but they can absorb any that leaks out. Released chemical essences, such as pheromones and endorphins, are their drugs, corresponding roughly to alcohol and heroin. Sweat is good, but tears are better, and sexual fluids are highly prized delicacies."

Ardie raised an eyebrow. "So you're telling us we're dealing with uglies that go bump in the night?"

Garry looked up at Ardie. "Revenants are vengeful ghosts," he said. "They always have an agenda. The fact that the present lord of the manor is in this castle does not bode well. It's possible that whatever spirit haunts this place is one of Lord Turcotte's ancestors who doesn't like how he's let the place go. This ghost may have designs on his lordship's life."

Gavin looked up from studying the floor between his shoes. "It sounds just as daft as it did back in my office, but I'm willing to listen to almost any theory. The head medical examiner can't find a cause of death for Cillian or Billy. They just stopped living."

"Scared to death?" Rhys ventured a guess.

"In that case, they would have had elevated levels of adrenaline at least," Ardie said.

"Not if the killer is a revenant," Rhys disagreed. "Dr. Arvel just told us they feed on our... secretions." Lord Turcotte looked around at the circle of eyes suddenly focused on him. "But I'm sure that I'm just pointing out the very obvious," he said.

"Not at all," Garry said. "That's a very astute observation. And it's possible the killings were just a ruse to lure you here."

Gavin shook his head. "I'm sorry. I just can't bring myself to believe in ghosts. At least not the sort that can kill someone by draining them. And while we're talking of it, are we laying the deaths of the salvage team members at the door of this 'vengeful ghost'?"

"It would be a very powerful revenant indeed that could drain someone of life," Garry said. "However, it's possible that the ghost might have tricked one of the men into doing something careless. Where is Tristan?"

"I haven't seen him for a while," Ardie said. "I've been trying to keep an eye on him, but it's been a hell of a day."

"A revenant would be irresistibly attracted to a liaison with Tristan's gift," Garry said.

"So what?" Rhys said. "As long as the lad's not off having a wank, he should be all right."

Bo winced at the nobleman's lack of tact as Ardie tried to make contact with Tristan's radio. The foreman stopped when they realized they could hear the radio beeping from Tristan's cot across the hall.

"Can't rationalize it, but I have a very bad feeling about this," Ardie said to Bo.

Bo nodded. "We'll start searching right now, and nobody goes alone. No explanations, no arguments, okay? Ardie, if you'll search this level with Sir Rhys, Dr. Arvel with me, and Gavin with... Where's Chris?"

"He went to make some phone calls," Lord Turcotte volunteered.

"Then we're looking for him too. Gavin, team up with Ardie and Sir Rhys. Ready, Dr. Arvel?" Bo asked.

Garry put down his cup and followed Bo up the stairs.

"I DON'T think I've been in this room," Tristan said as he leaned in the empty doorway.

"You can barely hear the storm in here," Chris said.

"We must be near the core of the building," Tristan said. "How's your torch?"

Chris turned his flashlight on and it emitted a strong beam of yellow-white light. "Seems good."

"I'm going to turn mine off, then," Tristan said. "It needs charging."

"That's a somewhat ironic statement, considering," Chris said.

"Considering what?" Tristan asked.

"Why we're here."

"You've lost me," Tristan said.

Chris's gaze shifted from Tristan's face to a spot just above his head. Tristan felt the vague pins and needles sensation that sometimes presaged the arrival of a spirit, and a spot on his right hand was growing warmer by the second. The young man looked down and tried to focus on his ring finger, but he couldn't see anything unusual. Chris, however, could clearly see a large gold ring set with a red stone that glowed like an ingot in the forge. Tristan took several calming breaths and ignored the burning pain in his hand. He felt the presence of a vastly powerful spirit, and it was important that he be collected when he faced it.

"You should go," Tristan said. "It could get dangerous in here."

"Not on your life," Chris smiled. "I wouldn't miss this for the world."

"You don't understand," Tristan tried again. "And I don't have time to explain, but the turmoil of the storm makes this a good time for the revenant to attack. So far he's been content to siphon energy, but...."

"I shall need much more of your energy, little one," Alun said as he materialized.

"I did as you asked, my lord," Chris said.

Alun glanced at the blond man. "You have done well, my minion, and you shall be rewarded. Serve me again by rousing the witch."

Chris looked into Tristan's eyes and smiled. "That will be my pleasure, my lord," he said.

Tristan didn't waste any more time being shocked. He spun and sprinted back down the corridor. He could feel the ghost's will hammering at his and knew he didn't dare open up and try to learn more about the revenant. Wisdom dictated a retreat until the weather calmed down. Chris leapt after Tristan, his outstretched fingers snagging in the young man's hair. Tristan yelped sharply at the sudden excruciating pain as Chris hauled backward. Pulled off balance, the liaison went down hard on his side, cracking his elbow and skull on the stone floor. Chris hooked his other hand under Tristan's armpit and dragged the stunned psychic back into the small chamber. Quickly, Chris pulled Tristan's pants down his hips, exposing the dark-pelted groin. Tristan fought, but couldn't dispel the grogginess from the blow to his head. Alun took advantage of the liaison's semi-conscious state to stimulate the pleasure centers of his brain. For as long as the psychic's barriers were down, the revenant's influence was nearly as limitless as it was in dreams.

Tristan groaned as his blurred vision swam into focus. The herbs the high priest had thrown into the Flames of Prophecy had left him with a worse-than-usual headache. He had no recollection of his visions, other than an impression of dark, damp stone walls, but a dull foreboding possessed him. He tried to rise and saw a golden-haired man in the chamber with him. The temple made a practice of buying the most exotic slaves the market offered, but the avatar had not seen this one before. He drew breath to inquire when someone spoke from behind him.

"Are you ready for your reward?" Alun asked his minion.

Chris nodded. "Yes, my lord."

"Very well," the revenant said, moving closer.

As Alun thrust his hand into Chris's chest and wrapped his fingers around the young man's heart, Tristan's distorted vision saw a Crusader plunge a dagger into a slave's heart. Chris fastened his eyes on Alun's in a wounded reproach that rapidly became utter horror as he felt his soul being drawn from him. The young man's knees failed, but the revenant kept him upright.

"You swore to serve me," Alun reminded him. "Your energy will give me the strength I need to take the witch. When I have filled him with my essence, nothing can stop my rebirth into the world of the living."

Chris's eyes went glassy as the last of the ineffable energy that animated him bled out into the revenant. The Crusader knight tossed aside the husk of his minion and fixed his glowing gaze on the paralyzed liaison.

"TELL me more about these revenants," Bo said as he and Garry entered the second floor's main corridor.

"I sense that you have a specific question in mind," Garry said.

Isn't he the clever one? Bo's little voice commented. Bo ignored his conscience and answered Garry. "Okay, I admit it, the sex stuff is fascinating. Call me a pervert. I'm sure I deserve it."

"Actually, your curiosity is quite normal for a mammal," Garry said. "Do you want to know if ghosts can have sex with the living?"

Bo smiled sheepishly. "Yeah, I guess I do," he said as he shone his light into another bare, windowless chamber.

"Most people are curious about that. Documented instances are so rare that I'm tempted to say no, but I believe it to be possible," Garry said. "Spirits are capable of planting erotic notions in our thoughts. Sometimes they can even impart a suggestive warmth to our flesh."

They reached the end of the hall, and Garry faced Bo.

"As far as actual penetration, which I'm guessing is what you really want to know, I've never heard of an authentic occurrence of intercourse between a human and a ghost. Ancient tales of incubi and succubi were mostly made up to cover up out-of-wedlock pregnancies."

"I always suspected that was the case," Bo said as they started up the next set of stairs. "You said the revenants feed on our fluids, that it makes them stronger."

"That's right," Garry said.

"You also said a revenant would be attracted to someone like Tristan."

"Let me put this in layman's terms," Garry said. "Tristan's energy field is to a revenant what the radiation of a yellow sun is to someone from the plant Krypton."

Bo's sandy brows rose at the comic book reference, wondering if the stern doctor was a secret fan of Superman, or if he just thought it was a frame of reference Bo could comprehend. "And what would happen if...?"

"If what?" Garry prompted as they reached the next level.

"If Tristan had sex in the castle, what would... what would the effect be?"

Garry gave Bo a sideways glance. "That's an interesting question. If my theory were correct, a revenant would want that more than anything. If a liaison as powerful as Tris were to climax within a revenant's sphere of influence, it would impart a very large amount of energy to the ghost. Along with all the attendant feelings of pleasure, magnified tenfold."

"Shit," Bo muttered.

"Is there something you'd like to tell me?" Garry stopped and met Bo's eyes.

THE earthly representative of the Goddess rose from the floor, wearing nothing but his long hair and henna tattoos. The Crusader took in the avatar's lissome form and appealing face. Purposefully, the big man strode across the room. The avatar wondered where his bodyguard was as the knight neared him. When no one appeared to help him, the young man shouted for the temple guards. At the sound of approaching footsteps, the Crusader drew his sword and turned toward the door of the chamber.

BO AND Garry looked in the direction of the desperate call for help and began moving toward it immediately.

"That was Tristan," Garry said unnecessarily.

"Bo!" Ardie shouted as he reached the top of the stairs at the other end of the hall, Rhys and Gavin behind him.

Tristan screamed and the four men broke into a run. Bo and Garry reached the room the shout originated from a step or two ahead of Ardie and Rhys. Ardie's gaze caught a tiny glint of light in the dark doorway and, instantly, the feeling of danger was so strong that Ardie reacted without stopping to question it. Flinging himself forward, he plowed into Bo, throwing his friend off his feet. As Bo fell against Rhys, the keystone of the arch dropped from its place with a loud crack. The wedge of stone swung forward, striking Ardie in the back, propelling him across the hall and pinning him there. The sickening sound of bones breaking was clearly audible, and blood began to pour from Ardie's nose and mouth. Bo was on his feet and at his partner's side in less than a heartbeat.

"Oh, no. Oh fuck no," Bo breathed.

Ardie cut his eyes at Bo, and Bo felt as though he'd grabbed hold of a wire with one hundred and ten volts of electricity running through it. Bo couldn't have looked away if he had wanted to. Putting a hand on Ardie's hair, he moved closer. Sir Rhys was staring at the handle of the stone pendulum that had swung from the arch and crushed Ardie. The stunned nobleman turned slowly from the ruin the booby trap had made of Andressen's second-in-command to look inside the chamber. Garry was with Tristan, speaking softly to the young man. Lord Turcotte looked back at Ardie and then cleared his throat.

"Dr. Arvel? Are you any sort of medical doctor or is it just... um, metaphysics?"

Garry took Tristan's hand and drew the young man with him from the chamber. "Watch him," the parapsychologist said tersely to Rhys.

Garry needed only a cursory look at Ardie to tell him there was no hope. He closed his eyes briefly before he spoke. "There's nothing to be done. I'm sorry."

"I kinda figured that, doc," Bo said. "Ardie, why can't you just tend to your own business?"

Ardie winked, and then he focused on the air to Bo's left. Bo's tears fell faster as Ardie tried to smile. "Hey," Ardie wheezed. "That's... weird. There's a guy...."

"Stop trying to talk," Bo said. "You're just making it worse."

Ardie lifted an eyebrow.

"It could hardly be any worse," Garry spoke Ardie's thought with uncanny accuracy. "And this is the last chance he'll have to say anything."

Tristan came to stand beside Garry. The liaison was shattered by what had just happened, but he gathered the shards of his courage and extended his gift. At once, he saw the silvery glow of Ardie's aura swirling about the man like a snow globe made from powdered stars. Tristan linked easily to Ardie's consciousness, absorbing some of the overwhelming pain and fear of death that the man was feeling. Their spirits meshed comfortably, if not perfectly, and Tristan was able to bring solace to the mortally injured man. As Tristan had suspected when they met, Ardie had a measure of the same talent he was gifted with.

"None... of this... is your fault," Ardie gasped out, his eyes on Bo.

"Shut up," Bo whispered, stroking Ardie's soft, dark hair.

"I wanted... this job, re... remember?"

"Fuck the treasure," Bo said. "Just don't die."

"Can't be helped," Ardie said.

Bo knew for certain then that his best friend was not going to be all right. Leaning heavily against the wall, Bo got as close as he could to Ardie.

"I love you," Bo said. "I hope you've never doubted that."

Ardie shook his head slightly. "Same ... goes for you," he said, a red bubble bursting on his lips.

"Jesus, Ardie," Bo said miserably as Ardie sagged.

"See you... later," Ardie breathed and the light in his eyes went out.

Bo pulled Ardie's forehead to his. "Not if I see you first," he whispered brokenly, and stood that way for a long time before he could force himself to let go of the dead man.

Gavin put away the radio that would bring no help; no boat, plane, or helicopter would be coming out in this storm. He moved to Bo's side and gazed at Ardie's body, his sharp eyes assessing every detail of the tragic scene. Without a word, he took hold of Bo's arm and turned him away. Rhys watched Tristan, as he'd been asked to do. The young man was gazing into the middle distance with the dreamy smile of an opium smoker. Rhys glanced at the group around the body and caught Garry's eye, nodding in Tristan's direction.

The parapsychologist came to stand in front of the young man, looking deep into the limpid stare. "Tristan?" Garry said softly. "Are you with us?"

There was no answer, and Rhys filled the silence. "Is he in shock?"

"Quiet," Garry said peremptorily. "And no, he's not in shock; he's... on his way back."

Lord Turcotte raised an eyebrow, but didn't comment as Garry took Tristan's hand and deliberately bent one of his fingers back. The nobleman winced, but the psychic didn't react at all. Frowning, Garry turned and called out.

"Mr. Andressen, would you come here, please?"

Bo shook off Gavin's support and walked over. Without being told, he reached for Tristan's hand and held it between his.

"Good," Garry said. "Now call him home."

Bo didn't ask questions, but did as directed. "Tris? Hey, kid, come on back now."

Lord Turcotte had counted to seven when the liaison's gaze sharpened and focused on his mentor. Immediately, the young man threw his arms around Dr. Arvel, like a child clutching at its mother's skirts.

"Garry," Tristan gasped. "It's a revenant."

CHAPTER TWELVE

"WHAT happened here, Dr. Arvel?" Lord Turcotte asked. "If you have an explanation, I'd very much like to hear it."

After caring for Tristan, Garry had escorted Rhys back into the main hall. Gavin and Bo took care of wrapping Chris Lukos's body in a blanket and plastic sheeting. Everyone was thinking about Ardie's remains, still trapped between the giant stone hammer and the wall upstairs. With the castle isolated by the storm, there was no hope of moving the massive stone to free the body. Garry poured himself a coffee from the carafe, but Turcotte declined. The nobleman sat like a little boy in a doctor's office, back straight, both feet flat on the floor, and hands folded neatly in his lap.

"It's a bit hard to explain," Garry said. "And it will sound more than a bit far-fetched, I'm afraid."

"Was it the ghosts?" Rhys asked bluntly.

Garry took a sip of the strong coffee to cover his surprise at the other man's instant acceptance of supernatural influences. "I believe so," he said. "One ghost in particular."

"Thank God," Rhys said, and Garry's eyebrows climbed toward his hairline. "I suppose that sounded a bit callous. I meant, thank God I'm not crazy. There really are monsters."

"I'm afraid there are," Garry nodded. "Terrible things they are too, some of them. Did you have a bad experience here?"

Rhys's eyes slid away from the other man's. "It was a long time ago," he said. "I was a child."

"I'd still like to hear about it," Garry said. "Think of it as professional curiosity."

"What about your… protégé? Doesn't he need you?"

"Tristan? He's been telling me for some time that he's grown-up, and as it turns out, he's right. It's a hell of a thing, though. He was just a wee curly-locked boy such a short time ago, and now he not only has power, but some of the maturity necessary to wield it."

"I see," Rhys said, though it was obvious that he didn't. "He'll be all right on his own then?"

"He's sleeping," Garry said, standing up. "Come on, Sir Rhys. We'll just go across this grand hall and over to the other side of that magnificent staircase. We'll be out of the line of sight of the others, and if we keep our voices low, no one will hear us."

Lord Turcotte hesitated, but Garry's calm, interested manner was soothing, and the nobleman really did want to talk about it. He nodded and followed the parapsychologist away from the center of the hall.

Tristan pulled back from the railing of the gallery on the right side of the great hall. He was glad Garry would be occupied for a while. There was something Tristan needed to do, and he knew his mentor would not approve. With quick, light steps, the liaison returned to the scene of Chris and Ardie's deaths. He didn't avert his gaze from the pitiful ruin of a beautiful, special man. The shell was empty; Ardie didn't live there anymore, and Tristan needed help to find his soul.

"There you are," the liaison said. "I thought I'd find you here. Time to stop slacking."

For a split second, Tristan saw an illusory vision of the hall as it had been centuries ago, with torches flaring on walls hung with jewel-toned tapestries, but it winked out of existence like a soap bubble bursting when the spirit spoke.

"I was just taking a break."

"Bullshit," Tristan said. "You're ducking out on your responsibilities, like you've been doing all along. No wonder you still haven't moved on."

"Fuck you, go-between."

"You might be the worst guardian I've ever seen," Tristan snapped.

"Report me."

Tristan could feel the waves of smugness coming from the spirit, and annoyance gave him the impetus he needed. Pushing aside all of his anxiety over his latest brushes with the supernatural world, Tristan summoned his gift and extended the thinnest of tendrils.

"It might be worth passing over to inform someone of the cock-up you've made of guiding Bo. He's supposed to be your ward," Tristan said. "You wouldn't be with him if he wasn't meant for a special purpose, a purpose that has probably been balked because of your negative attitude."

"Negative? I have only ever told him the truth," the spirit insisted.

Tristan sent another tendril to join the first, and then another and another, stretching toward the guardian like streamers of light. The spirit watched them come without concern as they twined together, becoming thicker and brighter.

"You only ever criticize him," Tristan said. "You never encourage him."

"And how would you know?"

Like a net of light, Tristan's gift enveloped the spirit, but it did not stop there. The shimmering motes of argent light passed through the surface of the translucent figure, becoming part of the guardian.

When the liaison lifted his hand, each separate spark flared with a brilliant radiance that merged until the spirit was visible.

"Now," the young man said. "Look at yourself."

With the power of his gift, and the strength of his will, Tristan forced the guardian to remember every damaging, destructive comment made to his charge. In the space between two heartbeats, the proud being stood with head drooping in shame.

"I know it's hard," Tristan said. "You're so superior to mortals in so many ways, and yet you're set to guard one like an indentured nanny. I don't have any answers for you. All I can tell you is that you'll be happier if you do your task well."

The guardian's shoulders were bowed and waist-length hair curtained the noble face. "I shall never Become."

Tristan moved forward, his gift rushing back to him like a film of a fireworks explosion run backward. "You're being negative again," he said. "Did you take a mortal name?"

"I call myself Jude."

"Jude, at the risk of making a bad pun, I can see right through you. You're more than capable of completing your task. You won't be here forever in this form. You'll do what you were meant to do and move on. You'll Become; you'll be born."

The spirit lifted a beautiful, sorrowing face. "You have seen inside me. You know of my great longing."

Tristan smiled. "Like all guardians, you want a body so you can affect the mortal world directly. You would right all the wrongs of this planet, if only you had a physical shell. Whispering in one man's ear is too slow a method of changing things."

"Yes! Exactly!"

"Jude," Tristan said. "I'm going to tell you a terrible secret. Everything you know is forgotten when you're born. It isn't lost, but it isn't accessible to the conscious mind."

"That isn't logical."

"I know. I wish I didn't know, but we all have our crosses to bear, if you'll forgive the expression."

"It just doesn't make sense."

"I know," Tristan repeated. "But when you're born, you'll be a blank slate with a whole new life as a thinking, feeling being, to do with as you wish. And you might have a little voice whispering in your ear. Someone frustrated, perhaps, that their assigned mortal won't listen to the wisdom they have to impart. Who knows? Maybe you'll listen."

The guardian straightened broad shoulders and met the liaison's eyes with new resolve. *"How can I help?"*

"I need a favor," Tristan said bluntly.

Jude perceived instantly what the liaison wanted. "I am forbidden."

"But not bound," Tristan pointed out.

"No, not bound, but if it were known...."

"You'd be righting a great wrong," Tristan said, glancing at Ardie's remains. "That's what drew you here, isn't it? You know this man's innocent soul is in thrall to the revenant. Free him. Let him move on."

"What if he doesn't move on once he's free?" Jude voiced the obvious flaw in Tristan's plan.

"Then I'll deal with him," the young man said. "Vengeful ghosts are my specialty."

"I'll do as you ask," the guardian said. "And I'll give you some advice. Have as much care for yourself as you do for others." With that, Jude was gone.

Tristan's shoulders slumped as though a heavy weight had fallen on them. He stood thus for long moments, absorbing the enormity of what he'd done, and then his head came up. He let his gaze circle the stone walls as the certainty that what he was doing was right settled on him like sunlight on his skin.

"I will not be afraid," he whispered as he waited.

BO FELT a breeze against his cheek that didn't smell of brine. He identified the faint scent as patchouli, and fresh tears overflowed. Ardie habitually wore patchouli oil instead of cologne. It was a scent at once exotic and down to earth, like the man himself. Rising, Bo looked aimlessly around. He couldn't seek solitude outside in the storm, nor did he wish to enter the dungeons. The higher reaches could only be accessed by the hall where Ardie's body remained. Left with few options, Bo entered the deconsecrated chapel. He walked up the short nave to the chancel and sat down. The fragrance of patchouli followed Bo into the sanctuary, evoking memories of his lost friend.

It would be impossible to forget his first sight of the half-breed kid whose test scores had won him a ticket off the reservation and into the accelerated program at Bo's high school. It wasn't so much the ragged clothes or the bad haircut that made him memorable, but the war paint smeared defiantly over his cheekbones. It became appropriate in less than an hour when Ardie punched a kid for calling him squaw boy. The taunter's friends joined in, and Bo had tried to even the odds a bit. He and Ardie had both got their asses kicked. *Some hero I was*, Bo thought. *Sorry, Ardie.*

He conjured a happier Ardie, in black leather with silver skull beads braided into his long, dark hair, choking the neck of a Fender guitar as feedback poured from the speakers. Bo on his knees in front of his lead guitarist, blond mane disheveled, bare chest gleaming with sweat as he howled the lyrics to a heavy metal anthem of the early eighties. The small crowd of college kids danced and screamed their heads off, fueled by beer, pot, and their love of the local cult band Cowboys and Engines. Bo shook his head in wonder that he had ever been that young. What had made him think that he could write original songs and have a recording career? Just as well that he had given it up when he did.

Bo sighed and moved on to mental snapshots of Ardie silhouetted against the Himalayas, a Bangkok temple, and on the banks of the Ganges during the year they traveled the East. They had talked about returning and using their new skills and the degrees conferred upon them at graduation to help the people of the primitive regions they had passed through. The dreams they built together around campfires in the middle of nowhere had been abandoned as they fell into careers. Had he ever really been that idealistic? How could they believe that two men could make any significant dent in the poverty-stricken conditions of the slums of India or Thailand? It had been a hash-pipe dream.

When Bo had grown sick of the construction business and conceived the romantic notion of hunting for treasure, he'd called Ardie. Ardie had left his Houston law firm, six-digit salary, and golden parachute to become Bo's partner. Even in the lean times—and there had been lean times—Ardie had never expressed a regret.

With his head in his hands, Bo sat, bereft and in despair, and recounted all his failures. He was a salvager, but he was damned if he could see what could be salvaged from this disaster.

Drawn by the depth of Andressen's pain, the revenant coalesced in the shadows to absorb the emanations of a soul in utter distress. Bo slumped farther, crumpling in on himself, folding under a weight too great for anyone to bear alone as the ghost greedily gobbled his despair. Sir Alun was about to summon his knights to the feast when he was interrupted.

"Back off, asshole."

The revenant stopped feeding as he was challenged. "You are in my thrall," he said. "You may not defy me."

"Fuck you and the Horse of the Apocalypse you rode in on, pard. Touch that man again, and I will waste you."

The revenant frowned in confusion at the other ghost's continued insubordination. "This mortal's soul is most potent. When I have absorbed his energy, I will be strong enough to take the witch and implant my essence."

"Which means fuck-all to me, Jack. We've laid our cards on the table. We already know what the stakes are. Do you want to up the ante again, or shall we see who's bluffing?"

"Interloper!" the Crusader's ghost warned. "Begone, or feel my wrath again."

"That's a hell of a comeback. As long as you're being all melodramatic, let me have a go at it. Fucketh off or thy ass I will kick."

Using some of the energy siphoned from Bo, the revenant released a ravening bolt of withering power that should have blasted the impudent apparition to floating rags. The look of surprise on Alun's noble features was almost comical when he beheld the other spirit still smiling cockily at him.

"Nice try, dicksmack," said the ghost of Sean Red Dog. "But I'm still standin'."

"Do not stand between me and my prey!"

"It's 'my prey and me'," Ardie corrected. "And anytime you want to tango, I'm ready."

"How is it you still defy me?" Alun demanded to know.

"That's for me to know and you to find out," Ardie taunted. "What you can be sure of is that if you even think of sucking off my friend again, you'll find me standing between you and him. And before you mention it, I know I can't beat you in a fair fight, so I'm not going to fight fair."

"I do not know how you escaped my thrall," Alun said. "But I will make you regret it, you insolent little...."

The revenant ceased blustering as Jude materialized at Ardie's side.

"So... whatta ya think of me now?" Ardie cocked an eyebrow at Sir Alun.

Alun saw Tristan in the doorway and a slow smile curved his lips. "Then let it begin," he said.

RHYS pressed the heels of his hands to his eyes and straightened his shoulders. His talk with Dr. Arvel had exhausted him emotionally, but he felt amazingly serene. Rising to his feet, he started to leave the gallery. Lord Turcotte found his way blocked by a handsome man whose garments were centuries out of date. The stranger didn't move an inch, and Rhys stopped to avoid colliding with him. The scant light reflected from the great hall glowed in deep, dark eyes as the strange man raised his eyes to meet Rhys's gaze.

"Where are you going?"

"Who are you?" Lord Turcotte asked. "And where did you come from?"

"My name is Sir Odilon, Sir Rhys. So you know you are dealing with an equal."

"What on earth are you babbling about?"

"What on earth?" Odilon grinned. "That's amusing, Sir Rhys."

"I've no time for your nonsense," Lord Turcotte said.

Odilon laughed, a sound both merry and sinister. "Time? You don't have anything else, my lord," the man said.

"Very well, then," Rhys said. "If you won't talk sense to me, come along and we'll let Constable Gilroy sort you out."

"You are going nowhere."

"Your lips don't move when you talk," Rhys said accusingly.

"I beg your pardon," Odilon said. "Is that better?"

"Who the hell are you?"

"I am Sir Odilon D'Aubigne, retainer to Sir Alun Turcotte."

Rhys's gaze narrowed as he turned the name over in his mind. "You're a ghost," he said.

"Aye, to be sure," Odilon said. "But we can still have fun, your lordship."

"What makes you think I want to have fun?"

"I thought a high sex drive might be a family trait." Odilon said with a grin. "You're going to be staying right here for quite a long time, Sir Rhys, so we may as well pass it pleasantly."

Rhys's eyes widened as the ghost seemed to grow until he was twice Rhys's height. However, when the man glanced around, he realized that it was he who had shrunk. He was no taller than a child of nine or ten. Rhys focused on the surroundings, and his heart began to beat faster. He was back in the dungeon, and the monster was here with him.

GAVIN woke, and his aching back told him he'd fallen asleep in the chair next to Tristan's cot. Looking about, the policeman realized he was alone, despite the agreement they'd all made to stay in sight of one another. He felt the unpleasant tickle of uneasiness and walked toward the staircase, looking for any sign of his companions. As he started up the left-hand steps, he caught a glimmer of light in the remains of the castle kitchens. Changing course, he snapped on his flashlight and followed the elusive glow.

"You shall not pass."

Gavin stopped dead in his tracks and goggled at the giant in his path. Gavin was used to being the biggest man in any room, but this fellow was easily six and a half feet tall with broad shoulders and long limbs. The policeman went for the handgun that he was never without since his rescue of Tristan all those years ago.

"I don't know who… or what you are," Gavin said. "But I will put holes in you if you don't start talking right now."

"I am Sir Richard of Alford, and I have the honor to be Sir Alun's champion. As such, I have the right to challenge you to single combat."

Gavin noted the way the beam of his flashlight streamed through the figure of the knight and how the big man's lips didn't move when he spoke. "You're not even real," Gavin said. "Why should I fear you?"

"My lance is long and made of good English steel," Richard said, dropping his eyes.

Gavin followed the ghost's gaze and saw that the codpiece was missing from the suit of armor. Sir Richard had removed one gauntlet and stroked his manhood with a leather-gloved fist. As he had boasted, the shaft was long and hard. Gavin would have found the entire scene a comic burlesque, but for the dread freezing his blood.

"You have the spirit of a warrior," the Crusader's ghost said. "I will take great pleasure in subduing you and bending you to my will."

"You may find that more difficult than you think," Gavin replied.

"That is my wish, also," Richard said with a smile. "There is no sport in taking women or silken harem boys. Thrusting my spear into an enemy who is doing his utmost to avoid the impaling is a challenge for a man."

"Bo! Dr. Arvel!" Gavin called. "Lord Rhys!"

There was no answer.

"They are otherwise engaged," the ghost said. "Have at you."

Gavin blinked in astonishment. The ghost, the kitchen, in fact, the entire castle was gone. He was standing in a horribly familiar alley, looking in a grimy window as a scarred thug terrorized a bound boy. Outrage flared in his blood, and he raised a fist to smash the glass.

GARRY became aware that someone was standing at his shoulder. Assuming it to be Lord Turcotte or the policeman, he ignored the presence for some time as he studied a page of the Book. Finally it impinged on his senses that he was inhaling the fragrance of myrrh, and his curiosity roused him.

"I beg your forgiveness," the ghost said, touching a translucent finger to the top of the page. "So the book was here all along. I cannot understand how I did not sense its presence."

Garry took in the voluminous robes of black silk, the masses of sable hair, and the inky eyes. "Who are you?" he asked in wonder.

"I am Aqil Abd al-Aziz, the author of this particular passage."

Garry's eyes widened. "This is incredible."

"Of course, I am in truth only the essence of the one who was called Aqil," the ghost said. "But it makes little difference what you call me."

"You've no idea how much I've wanted to talk with someone like you, and now that I have the opportunity...." Garry shook his head. "Are you in league with the revenant?"

"Do not let that concern you," Aqil said as several shots rang out. "Let me show you some of the mysteries you have been so curious about."

CHAPTER THIRTEEN

BO SHOOK off his grief as Tristan came into the chapel. "What's going on?" the salvager asked, jumping to his feet.

Tristan ignored Bo. "You were supposed to move on," he said to the middle distance between the other man and himself.

"Move on where?" Bo asked in confusion.

Tristan focused on him. "Sorry, I wasn't talking to you. We don't have a lot of time for explanations. Anyway, you've had them already from Garry, you just don't believe them. Would you just take my word that you're in great danger?"

"From who or what?" Bo asked skeptically.

"There are ghosts in this chapel with us."

"Really?" Bo said. "And I suppose there's no way for you to prove it."

"Of course there is, but to make them visible, I would have to give the bad ones more power."

"You make it sound so plausible," Bo said. "I surely do want to believe that my friends didn't die just because Fate was feeling capricious. But…." Bo stopped speaking as a warm wave of passion swept through him. He saw Tristan's lips moving and heard the liaison's words, but they were as meaningless and soothing as waves lapping at the shore. With a kindling smile, Bo moved toward the young man.

Tristan easily divined Bo's intentions as he watched the man walk through Ardie's spirit without seeing or feeling it. "Are you going to do something about this?" the liaison asked Bo's guardian.

Jude shrugged. "He likes you. I think loving you would be a positive thing for him."

Before Tristan could retort, the guardian turned from him to face Sir Alun.

"You know my power," the revenant sneered.

Jude nodded. "I know. I just don't care anymore. I am a guardian; I shall guard."

"So be it." Sir Alun gestured imperiously, and Richard and Odilon materialized from thin air to stand before him.

"What is your will, my lord?" Richard asked, glowering at Jude.

"Have you done as I commanded?" Alun asked.

"Aye, my lord. The other mortals will not trouble you," Richard answered.

"They are wrapped in dark dreams," Odilon smiled.

"And the Saracen, where is he?" Alun demanded.

"I know not," Richard said.

"He spoke of finding the grimoire, my lord," Odilon said.

Alun frowned. The book of spells would be theirs along with everything else in the castle, once they completed the ritual. He had given Aqil no orders to search for it. For the first time, he seriously considered the possibility that one of his minions might betray him. It had never occurred to him that the Saracen would act against his own interests, no matter how much he resented the Crusader. Aqil stood to gain as much or more than Alun when they rejoined the world of the living. Alun would regain all his possessions, but Aquil would return with all his arcane knowledge intact. And with the grimoire.

"What would you bid me do now?" Richard said, seeing the sudden change in his liege's expression.

"Rid me of these gnats that plague me," the revenant commanded, pointing at the guardian and Ardie's ghost.

"Gladly, my lord," Richard said.

Jude took Ardie's metaphysical hand. "Don't be afraid," the guardian said. "I'll take care of you."

Ardie nodded. "I don't care what happens to me. But I won't let that smug asshole use Bo again. And I don't care how long this Alun character's been around. There's a limit to respecting your elders."

"Agreed," Jude said. "Let them come. Though we will surely be destroyed, we shall make them regret it."

"Always the optimist," Tristan said softly past the tightness of his throat.

Bo reached for Tristan, and the liaison did nothing to resist the man's amorous advances; there was no point. The revenant held them in his power for now. However, that power would have to wane eventually, and then Tristan would be able to break free. All he had to do was keep from panicking and trust in his allies.

"Excellent," Alun said as Bo nuzzled at Tristan's collarbones. "When this warrior has brought you to release, I will have the power I need to finish the ceremony that was broken all those centuries ago. This is not as I had planned, but in a campaign one must sometimes be bold and seize the opportunity."

"I'll never surrender to you," Tristan said.

"Then I will take you by force," Alun said matter-of-factly as Bo's hand slid under Tristan's shirt.

Tristan could no longer ignore his body's responses to Bo's caresses. His warm flannel shirt was peeled up and Bo paid court to his nipples, licking and sucking ardently. Tristan gave a soft groan as teeth came into play.

"Yes," Alun purred. "Catch fire, my beauty. Tonight you will know delights that few mortals are privileged to taste."

"My power and my will are as great as yours," Tristan said in a clear, steady voice. "I'll send you from this plane, so you can find rest."

"You are a formidable opponent," Alun said. "But flesh is so fragile... so easily bruised, or torn, or smashed to jelly."

"Bastard!" Tristan said.

Alun's black look reminded Tristan that his insult had been more serious in the Crusader's day. "Proud fool," the revenant replied. "You think you know the rules, but you are playing the wrong game. It is not my will that holds you powerless. You are bound by the Saracen's spell. You can do nothing to hinder me, and soon your allies in my realm will be gone as well."

Tristan's gaze didn't leave the revenant; he could feel the truth of the specter's words. The ghost knights were slowly consuming Ardie and Jude's essences. The two brave spirits bought time for Tristan, but they were diminishing fast. Tristan's gamble would doom them all if he had been wrong in even one of his calculations. Clutching desperately at his eroding self-confidence, the liaison tried once again to connect.

"Soon," the revenant gloated, as Bo's hand slid under the waistband of Tristan's loose pants. "You cannot resist this man's touch now anymore than you could nine hundred years ago. You were willing to risk your life to be in his arms then, but this time you shall not die. You shall live, and you will be my bridge back to the waking world."

Tristan experienced the curious sensation of his blood running hot and cold at the same time, from Bo's attentions and the revenant's intentions. The psychic wanted to pass the ghost's words off as delusions, but the revenant had caused Ardie's death, and who knew how many others? Sir Alun's threats were not empty ones. For the first time in a decade, Tristan felt the bleakness of despair. He couldn't do this alone; he needed help.

Garry entered the chapel and looked around. "I had the strongest feeling that you needed me," the parapsychologist said, and then his eyes fell on the revenant. "I can see you clear as day," he exclaimed.

Sir Alun's ghost was patently not expecting visitors. "Who are you, mortal?" the revenant demanded.

"I'm the invisible man," Garry said with a sardonic smile. "Your sort can't sense me from a distance. I'm as nonexistent to you as you are to most mortals."

The revenant's eyes narrowed. "Richard, my lion, finish what you are doing and fetch the Saracen, damn his black eyes."

"I think we may agree to a temporary truce, Sir Alun," Garry said as he slid a look at Tristan. "I can see you're busy, Tris, but would you mind telling me why you're allowing this bedsheet to make you perform a live sex show?"

Two patches of rose appeared over the young man's high cheekbones. "This isn't extraordinary, considering the level of manifestation we're dealing with here. There's something more at work here than a simple emotion-generated haunting."

"Perhaps if you didn't look like you were enjoying it quite so much," Garry said dryly, "it would be easier to believe that you're outmatched. I assume Mr. Andressen is unaware of our conversation?"

"I think he's unaware of pretty much everything but me," Tristan answered.

"What's the scenario?" Garry asked.

"It involves a temple. I don't know the deity, but the setting is vaguely Persian, Eastern anyway. Bo's a Varyag barbarian hired as a guard. I'm a figurehead of some sort, as far as I can tell, a sort of priest who's also a proxy for the Goddess. Mr. Red Dog, Ardie, was the high priest of this cult. The revenant—" Tristan gasped as Bo sucked hard on his nipple while firmly stroking his lengthening shaft. There was a slight tremor in the liaison's voice when he resumed speaking. "The revenant is the ghost of Sir Alun Turcotte. He's the knight sacking the temple in my vision."

Garry looked askance at the tableau of his protégé being fondled by the enthralled treasure hunter. He didn't understand why Tristan didn't break the malicious spirit's control over him. The revenant was powerful, but Tristan was too, and he knew better than to play into the ghost's game. "Tristan," Garry tried again. "Why are you still submitting to the delusion when you've recognized it? It has no power over you. Snap out of it."

Tristan didn't answer. It was hard to talk with two tongues in your mouth. Bo wrapped his arms around the young man and lowered him to the chancel floor as the kiss continued. Going to his knees, Bo worked Tristan's trousers down his hips, freeing his arousal.

"All right, that's quite enough," Garry said. "What's the revenant's hold over you, Tris?"

The apparition's smoldering gaze watched Garry approach the pair rutting under his influence. Sir Alun had not agreed to a truce, but he could get no sense of this wizard's powers and was loath to risk attacking him without Aqil there.

Bo bowed his head over Tristan's shaft as Garry leaned down. Tristan wove his fingers into Bo's straw-colored hair and moaned his approval of the man's technique. Doing his best to ignore what was happening under his nose, Garry searched for a talisman on Tristan. Tristan's soft moans became cries of pleasure as Bo lavished attention on his balls, his perineum, and his quivering erection. The young man clutched fistfuls of pale hair as Bo drove him delirious.

The red gem on his finger gleamed like fresh blood in the dim light, catching Garry's eyes. Garry had never seen the ring before, and the only jewelry Tristan ever wore was a necklace Alicia had given him. Tristan was not given to adornment, and Garry doubted the ring was a gift. The gem was cabochon cut, suggesting antiquity, and appeared to glow with its own light, hinting at arcane tampering.

"No!" the revenant roared as Garry reached for the signet.

Certain now that he'd found the amulet that hampered Tristan's ability to link, Garry tugged at the gold circlet. The liaison took no notice as a wet tongue entered his sheath.

"Hang on, Tris," Garry said. "I'll have this evil thing off you in moment."

Tristan heard his mentor's voice as an echo of thunder from the storm outside the castle and the storm that raged within him. Grain by grain, the malachite walls of the ancient temple materialized around him. He felt the cool solidity of Her altar beneath him. The mouth and hands of his barbarian lover drew him further into reckless abandon. Garry's words were the cawing of storm crows as Tristan was subsumed by the past.

Too late, Garry heard a stealthy footfall behind him and started to turn. A wooden oar slammed into the side of his head, dropping him to his knees. The first blow was swift and brutal, and the second was no different. Garry measured his length on the flagstones and didn't move. Satisfied, the attacker rose from a feral crouch and faced the ghost.

"Welcome," the revenant said. "You come in good time. I need to be elsewhere."

Chapter Fourteen

DROPPING his shirt to the floor, Bo lifted his lover to the altar. He felt no sacrilege in the act. They were going to celebrate life with their joining. Surely the Goddess could not be displeased. The warrior gazed with longing on the lean-muscled body of the avatar, sprawled wide-legged on the black stone. He leaned forward to take the lips offered up to him, but stopped a breath away.

"What's going on here?" he asked.

"We're in the past," Tristan said. "Or at least a version of it. Mine, yours, the revenant's, I don't know. Maybe it's a composite. But we're trapped in it, sure enough. I'm a little surprised that you're aware of the regression. You weren't before."

"And you were?"

"Of course."

"And you didn't tell me what was going on?"

"Don't get angry, please."

"How could I not be angry? I had a right to know if… if ghosts were… were… doing whatever it is they're doing to me."

Tristan cocked an eyebrow at Bo and sat up on the altar with his feet dangling. "And if I had told you, you would've believed me? I don't think so. And the reason I want you to stay calm is because the revenant feeds on emotions as well as sexual energy."

Bo took a deep breath. "I happen to think I'm incredibly calm considering the circumstances."

"You have a point, but I don't have time to go into detail right now. I'll wager anything you like that Sir Alun comes through that archway very soon with nothing but bad intentions. You, being my guard, will draw your weapon, but too late. The knight will run you through and ravish me on this altar."

"And that was supposed to happen last night, but Ardie got in the way," Bo guessed.

"I believe so," Tristan said. "It's what the revenant is trying to relive. I wish we'd had the chance to get to know one another before this Dark Ages Darth Vader hijacked us. Believe it or not, I respect you, and I think that, well, under different circumstances, we'd be...." Tristan paused and then spoke again. "For what it's worth, I'm sorry I didn't tell you. If I had it to do over again, I'd like to think I would trust you."

"Is that what you gifted people call an apology?" Bo said wryly. "So what happens after I die, and you get...."

Bo found himself incapable of uttering the word "rape." He was abruptly sick with rage at the very thought of Tristan defiled by some vicious attacker. It would not happen; he would not allow it. He would slay any who dared.

"You feel it," Tristan said.

"I felt like someone else for a second, if that's what you mean," Bo said. "Someone used to settling things with violence."

"It helps if you think of yourself as a channel," Tristan said. "Most people can't fully access the memories of their past, they only get muffled echoes. But when I'm linked to a spirit, I sometimes experience a memory from a past life of mine from that same era. I wish I could make you understand how amazing it is that you're aware of this memory."

"I find it more amazing that we knew each other in the past and met again," Bo answered.

Tristan smiled fondly at the man. "You're incredible," he said. "You're taking this all in stride, and you're using your brain instead of waiting for someone else to think for you."

Bo snorted. "Are you hitting on me again?" he asked.

Tristan laughed, the merry sound echoing off the malachite walls of the temple. "If we live through this, I definitely want to know you better," the psychic said.

"Suits me. We've already got that awkward 'when do we sleep together' thing out of the way. Might as well get engaged."

"Americans," Tristan said. "Always in a hurry. I'm going to court you, so brace yourself."

"Good advice," Sir Alun said as he strode into the chamber.

"Shite!" Tristan cursed. "He's early."

Bo put his hand on his sword as Alun lunged.

PIVOTING in a circle, the injured man took in the seam of the ceiling and walls of the room, trying to figure out just where he was. He had no idea how long he'd been unconscious, but he could feel a lump the size of a Volkswagen on his forehead, and his memory was a sometime thing. He was on the verge of going back out into the gloomy corridor when his gaze flickered once more over the smoke-blackened frieze that ran around the top of the walls.

He frowned at the repeated pattern of a hunting scene. Surely the carvings depicting a stag brought to bay by horsemen and hounds were an odd choice for a dungeon room, more suited to a banquet hall or audience chamber. Standing in the space between the onrushing horses and the kneeling stag was an archer with an arrow nocked—four identical hunts frozen in time, one per wall. He examined each of the tiny hunters, but nothing caught his eye until he looked again and saw that one of the archers had already loosed his bolt.

With the strong feeling that this meant something, he scanned the walls again, but the throbbing in his head would not allow him to form complete thoughts. His frustration mounting, he pressed his palms to the sides of his head and shouted just to hear a voice. At the sound of several running footsteps, he spun toward the entrance. Gavin Gilroy appeared in the arched opening and stared in shock.

"James!" the policeman exclaimed as Lord Turcotte pushed past him to get to the injured man.

James blinked, and the recent past flooded back. "Oh my God. Constable Gilroy. How did you find me?"

Gavin hurried over to took at the linguist's injuries as well. "You were presumed dead," he said with a grimace as he gingerly touched the goose egg on James's forehead.

"I feel like I've just crawled out of my grave," James said. "I was in the dark for so long, I thought I must be in hell, and I can tell you that an eternity of wandering lost through dank tunnels is enough to convince me to live right from now on."

"That's the damnedest thing," Gavin said. "I was also lost in the dark. I had a nightmare about an old case, at least I think it was a nightmare, but it felt like I was really back there in the past. Only this time, it happened differently. Instead of me rescuing the victim, the kidnappers captured me and.... Well, it was downhill from there. Let's just say they found some very inventive ways to make me suffer before I passed out. But a dark man dressed like an extra from the *Arabian Nights* woke me up and told me to come here. And then—laugh if you like—he disappeared. In a puff of smoke."

"Me too," Rhys put in. "I had a… different nightmare, but the same fellow woke me and directed me here. I met up with Constable Gilroy at the top of the stairs."

"I don't understand," James said, rubbing the bridge of his nose.

"Do you know about Gryffud?" Gavin asked hesitantly.

James's eyes filled with tears. "I remember the explosion. Is Gryf gone?"

"I'm afraid so, lad," Gavin said. "He'd have felt nothing, if that gives you comfort."

James nodded jerkily, and there was silence for several long moments before Rhys spoke.

"Shouldn't we try and find everyone else? It seems logical that if we were attacked, the others are in danger too."

"Yes, of course," Gavin took hold of James's arm. "Lean on me," he said.

"Wait," James resisted the pull toward the doorway. "Who are we in danger from?"

"Don't laugh," his lordship said. "But it seems as though the ghost of my ancestor has taken exception to our presence here."

"I'm not laughing," James said. "And until someone proves differently, I'm going to operate on the theory that this is a haunted castle."

Gavin shrugged. "I'll not hinder you," he said.

"Then give me a few more minutes here. I've reason to believe we'll find something that will be a weapon against the… evil spirit," James answered. "There was a passage in the Big Ass Book about a dagger, a dagger important enough to have a name, *Al Clavo*. It's my theory that the knife was sacred to the temple that Sir Rhys's ancestor plundered to amass his fortune. It was bound with spells and hidden away somewhere in these dungeons. The Book gave instructions for finding it again, but, of course, they were in code. Arrows were—"

The linguist broke off as Sir Rhys went to the west wall like a sleepwalker. Turning to face the room, he put his shoulders against the damp stone and slid down to a squatting position. "I was a lot shorter then," the nobleman muttered as he turned his head to the left.

James crouched beside the wall and followed the direction of Lord Turcotte's gaze. In between the stone blocks of the fifth row up, a series of arrows was scratched, like a dotted line. James duckwalked forward to put his palm on one of the rectangular stones. As he touched it, a smile lightened his face.

"Watch this," the linguist said and pressed hard against the bottom seam where the block rested atop another.

The stone pivoted inward and upward, permitting light to enter the cavity beyond. No chamber full of treasure lay beyond, however. The depression was little more than a handspan deep and contained one object a little over a foot long.

"Aren't you clever?" Gavin whistled.

James carefully lifted out the narrow, oblong cedar box. The linguist finessed the twists of gold wire out of the hook and eye closures and opened the coffin-shaped casque. Inside was an oiled leather pouch laced with thongs of waxed sinew.

"Heavy," the linguist remarked. "If this isn't a dagger, I'll eat it."

"You're going to feel awfully foolish if that's a crucifix," Gavin remarked.

James unwrapped several swaddling layers of rotting silk and bared a needle-slim blade with an ornate hilt and a crossguard shaped like a crescent moon. The handle was ivory, wrapped with gold wire and set with large dark red stones.

"It's a poignard," James said, holding up the dagger. "You can see the blade would be triangular in cross section. A weapon meant for one purpose—to punch through something."

"Skulls or breastplates, one assumes," Rhys said. "Now we've found it, what exactly do we do with it?"

"We slay the dragon," Gavin guessed.

"Manticore," James corrected. "Sorry, but as Sir Rhys can attest, the family crest has a manticore on it, not a dragon."

"You intellectuals will quibble in the path of a lava flow," Gavin said. "How is that important at the moment?"

"It isn't really," James said as he stood. "But why be ignorant?"

"I know I'm just a plodding constable," Gavin answered. "But how do you kill someone who's already dead?"

"I don't know," James admitted. "But if my friends are in trouble, I've got to try and help them."

"Good lad," Gavin said. "I'm with you."

Lord Turcotte hesitated only a moment before throwing in with them. It was the first time in his life he'd felt part of something; these men treated him as an equal, not a superior, and he found that he liked it. With a sense of purpose he'd not felt before, the nobleman followed his companions up the tumbled stairs.

THE revenant Crusader's broadsword thrust at Bo's unprotected side, but the steel never found its target. A spear with a leaf-bladed tip caught the sword and flung the weapon back. Sir Alun stared in amazement at the Celtic warrior facing him.

"Your minion made a wee mistake in killin' me," Morgan's ghost said. "He didn't stop to think how much power he was givin' me by freein' me from that whiskey-sodden sack o' flesh. Now, you lingerin' bad odor, I'm goin' to freshen the air a wee bit."

Alun glared at Morgan. "Begone," the revenant said. "You have no power here."

"You wish," Morgan replied. "I will not let you harm either of these men without it costin' you dear. So you decide, your lordship."

Morgan planted himself squarely in front of Bo and Tristan and raised his shining spear. As though he'd been blown out like a candle, the Crusader vanished.

JAMES, Gavin, and Rhys strode into the chapel and froze like children walking in on their parents having sex. Bo and Tristan were half-clothed and entwined. Garry lay on the floor, bleeding from a head wound. Standing in the middle of the nave, watching the oblivious couple, was a dark-cloaked figure.

"Vicar!" Gavin exclaimed. "How did you get here?"

"With great difficulty," Sean Carnes answered, his gaze lighting on the dagger. "My, that's a remarkable example of medieval Moorish craftsmanship. Do I assume you've found the treasure?"

The sight of his boss making love to the young psychic as if they were the only two people in the room transfixed James. Rhys stared as well, rendered speechless. It was left to Gavin to question the priest.

"You haven't answered my question," the policeman said. "Why are you here, Vicar?"

"You asked *how* I got here," Carnes observed. "Which is it?"

"I'll have both," Gavin said without a trace of humor.

"Oh dear," the vicar said. "Someone's moody."

"I have good reason," Gavin said. "I want answers from you, and, clergyman or not, they had better be good ones."

"Open your eyes, Gavin," the vicar said. "There are miracles all around you. I'm here to be present at one of them. Tonight, my Lord will be reborn."

Rhys joined the conversation. "When you say 'my Lord', are you speaking of Jesus Christ?"

The vicar chuckled. "Hardly. I have never worshiped the Shepherd. The Christian faith is for weaklings. I am a pagan, and my Gods don't turn the other cheek."

"You played us all for fools," Gavin said. "Tell me, how does a person live in a community and act as its minister while carrying out a series of murders? I've always wondered that when I read about men like Dahmer or Bundy. How do you do it and live with yourself?"

"He doesn't have a conscience, obviously," Rhys said flatly.

"I don't need one," Carnes said. "The past is gone, the future doesn't exist. It's only what I do right now that matters."

"That's very nice for you," Gavin said. "What about everybody else?"

"Only those with great will and courage can follow this path," the vicar said.

"And what's waiting at the end of it?" Rhys asked.

"In my case, immortality," Carnes answered. "I'll never be sick, and I'll never look any older than I do now. What would that be worth to you, your lordship? If it only cost a few lives, you'd pay the price, wouldn't you? Countries spend lives for mere commodities like oil. How many would you spend if you could live forever?"

"You're asking the wrong man," Rhys said. "Eternal life sounds awful to me."

"That makes you one of the sheep," the vicar said. "There's no shame in it. Everything in life has a purpose."

"What a load of shite!" Gavin exclaimed. "Vicar, you're under arrest for the murders of William Nye, Cillian Pryce, and Chris Lukos to start. You can be sure it won't end there."

"How did I kill them?" Carnes challenged.

"That's for the forensics people to find out," Gavin said. "And no doubt some psychiatrist will find out why you sacrificed these young men to your pagan idols. All I have to do is arrest you."

"It isn't me," the vicar said. "I didn't kill anyone. Well, no one except for Morgan, but he'll hardly be missed and his end was peaceful and painless."

Gavin's jaw dropped at this candor.

"I believe that's what people in your line of work call a confession," Rhys said to Gavin.

"Yes, thank you, I actually heard him say that," Gavin said. "If you didn't kill the boys, Vicar, who did?"

"You'll see," Carnes said with a superior smirk. "He's busy with the lovebirds right now, but you'll meet him, never fear."

"You're stark raving mad," Gavin told the vicar.

"You'd like to believe that," Carnes said. "But you and Sir Rhys have already met two of the ghosts. You should've succumbed to them and been put neatly out of the way, so I'll assume the wizard finally turned coat, as I told my lord he would."

"Wizard?" Rhys repeated. "Would that be the Harry Potter or the Gandalf type of wizard?"

"Mock me," the vicar said, "I don't care. When Sir Alun returns...."

Everyone turned to stare as a large man materialized between them and Bo and Tristan. "My lord," Carnes called out exultantly.

The revenant glowered at his minion. "Why did you slay the Celt?"

"For you," Sean Carnes said. "To remove an obstacle from your path."

"Fool! You have given him the power of a guardian. I must waste precious energy to subdue him, and I shall require more."

"No, my lord," the vicar screamed as the revenant flowed over him. "I did it for you. You would not punish me for serving you?"

Alun snarled. "You are a tool, nothing more, and right now you can best serve me by feeding me."

"No!" Carnes shrieked as the revenant sank translucent fingers into his skull.

The vicar dangled from the ghost's hold, twitching feebly as Alun sucked every scintilla of energy from him. Letting the limp, lifeless shell fall to the floor, the brightly glowing revenant swept the room with his gaze.

"Flee or stay," the Crusader's ghost intoned. "When I return, you will all die."

Chapter Fifteen

"SURRENDER!" Sir Richard's ghost raged at the stubborn spirits of Ardie and the guardian.

The battle invisible continued unabated. There was no swordplay, no punches thrown, only the unrelenting struggle of will against will, fueled by precious life force energy.

"Bah! This is exhausting our reserves," said the ghost of Sir Odilon. "We need the Saracen."

"I do not think we can count on the magus's help," Richard said sourly. "Let us destroy these two as our Master wishes. The guardian is weak, and the other is a novice."

"It's over," Jude the guardian said quietly. "I can no longer shield us—they are strong with the energy they stole from your friends. When my will fails, they will consume us."

"Isn't there any other way?" Ardie asked. "When we're gone, these two spooks are going to go for Bo and the kid."

Jude looked deep into the eyes of Ardie's ghost and then dropped his gaze.

"What?" Ardie prompted. "You thought of something, but you don't want to do it, right? Yeah, I'm right. If you know something that could help, you'd better tell me what it is."

The guardian bowed his head. "I could give up my post here. It's within my power to relinquish guardianship and return home. But if I do, I might wait a long time for another chance to prove myself worthy of being born."

"You're a guardian," Ardie said. "So guard."

Jude looked past Ardie at Tristan and Bo and returned his attention to the ghosts of the Crusaders. The guardian did not see how abandoning his charge helped him live up to his responsibilities, but he would have to go on faith now. He had nothing else left.

"Ardie," the guardian said. "Take my hand, and I will try to draw you with me."

"Screw that," Ardie said, throwing his arms around Jude and holding tight. "Do what you gotta do, and don't worry about me. I'll hang on and try not to cramp your style."

"I'll wait for them to link completely with me," Jude said. "It's my hope that by leaving, I can pull them away from here."

"Sounds good to me," Ardie said, glancing over at Bo. "I'm going to miss a few things here, though."

"Say farewell and look your last," the guardian advised him.

NO TIME at all had passed in the ancient temple between Sir Alun's departure and his return. The glowing ghost, replete with the vicar's energy, appeared in the shrine and moved toward the other three souls.

"So you've come back," Morgan said. "And I thought you'd run off with your tail between your legs. I warn you: I'll not let you desecrate the Goddess's sacred altar."

"You don't possess the power to stop me," Alun sneered.

"I'll have a go at it anyway, if it's all the same to you, boyo," Morgan answered.

"You cannot change what happened in the past," the Crusader said.

"I already have, just by bein' here," Morgan told him. "And this isn't exactly the past, now, is it? It's just your memory of it, you big bastard. Take another step toward the altar, and I'll spit you like a goat."

Bo stood at the Celt's shoulder, his short sword in one hand and the long blade in the other. Tristan stood just behind the shrine, sweeping aside the altar cloth to get at the coffer where the ceremonial objects were stored.

"Go," Morgan said to Bo. "Take the avatar and flee this place. Keep him safe—the Goddess loves him well."

"I'll not run from a fight," Bo declared, his eyes kindling with berserker fury.

"You will," Morgan said, his eyes on Alun. "For Tristan's sake. You must take him far from here and leave this shite in a tin can to me. I'm a guardian, too, you know."

Bo felt Tristan's light touch between his shoulder blades, letting him know the young man was there but out of the way of the warriors' weapons. The contact triggered a frisson of premonition that jarred Bo back to awareness of his present self. Sheathing his short sword, Bo reached back and grasped Tristan by the wrist.

"Come on," he said. "We're getting the hell out of here."

Alun sneered, resting the point of his sword on the floor and leaning on the hilt to illustrate how confident he was. "As I told your friends, flee or stay, it makes no difference. I will kill you and plunder this place. An army of knights is sacking this city as we speak. I was canny enough to find this heathen temple with all its riches, both tangible and intangible."

Bo edged to his right, pulling Tristan with him.

"No," Tristan said. "We can't let him defile Her temple."

Bo risked a look at the psychic. The young man's eyes were almost all pupil. In one hand, he held a needle-bladed dagger encrusted with jewels.

"It's only a building," Bo said carefully. "You're an avatar. I'm not sure exactly what that is, but I'm willing to bet it's more important than any pile of rocks."

"Listen to Bo," Morgan told Tristan as Alun raised his sword. "You are the Goddess's altar, not this cold slab of stone. It will never quicken with the spark of divinity, but you will. Go and keep Her worship alive."

Bo shook his head, as confused as one man could possibly be. Was it now? Or then? Was Morgan's ghost in the past? Were any of them sane? Was this a chemically induced hallucination? Was he still asleep on the plane to Wales?

"Go," Morgan commanded, keeping Alun at bay with his spear.

Bo tugged on Tristan's arm, but the young man wouldn't budge.

"The three of us can defeat him," the avatar said.

"He's wearing a full suit of armor," Bo pointed out. "And his friends are on their way."

"I will not leave so that this can happen again," Tristan answered. "Help me, please."

Bo hefted the weapon in his hand. He'd never had occasion to hold a real sword and was pretty sure there was more to it than just swinging it around. He felt far from confident about his chances against a battle-hardened Crusader.

"Go!" Morgan shouted furiously as he parried another hammering blow of the big knight's broadsword. "Or do I risk my soul for nothing?"

"Not for nothing," Tristan cried. "Together we will slay this monster that would trample everything the Goddess represents."

"Stubborn git, this is why you always die," Morgan growled as he fended off a flurry of strikes.

Tristan turned his head, pulled Bo sharply toward him, and welded his mouth to the other man's. A rush of heat like dragon's breath burned away the thin veneer of civilization that separated the salvager from the savage. For the sake of defending love and honor, Bo consciously surrendered to the traces of the mercenary warrior that remained in his genetic code. Pulling the buckler from its sheath again, Bo held both blades competently. Instinctively, his posture changed as he resettled his weight, coming on guard. With a glance, he herded the young man behind him. Tristan crouched in the warrior's shadow, one hand resting lightly on his defender's back.

Alun got a look at the dagger in the young man's hand and called for his vassals.

STANDING spellbound in the ancient chapel's nave, James held the ancient dagger in a white-knuckled grip. He stared raptly at the couple on the chancel floor where the altar used to be as he listened intently. Maybe he was going mad, but he could swear he heard Ardie's voice. Shaking his head in an attempt to clear it, Chris turned to Gavin.

"Do you hear anything strange?" James asked.

Gavin moved from his kneeling position beside Garry's body to the vicar's still form. "Everything here is strange," Gavin said. "Looks like these two are past help. Is anyone going to say anything to them?" The policeman pointed his chin at Bo and Tristan.

"Useless," Rhys reported as he rose from his crouch beside Bo and Tristan. "They don't hear or see anything but each other. Whatever they've been drinking, I need a shot."

"Quiet!" James hissed. "Listen."

The chapel fell silent save for the small sounds made by the lovers. Several seconds went by before Rhys spoke again.

"That's the wind," Lord Turcotte said. "It sounds like voices sometimes as it blows through the castle. Used to scare flaming hell out of me when I was a lad."

"No, it's not the wind, it sounds like... Ardie," James said and waited for the ridicule.

Neither of the other men laughed. Gavin met James's eyes and cocked his head like a curious hound. Rhys looked from one to the other, waiting for someone to do something.

"Good-bye, Ardie," James murmured.

"Safe journey, Ardie," Gavin said solemnly. "I wish I'd known you better."

Sir Rhys bade Ardie farewell also, feeling more than a little foolish.

"How touching," Odilon said to Richard. "Perhaps we should show ourselves so they can see what befalls their comrade."

Richard frowned. "We should not waste the energy to become visible. Come, brother, let us destroy these upstarts once and for all."

Richard and Odilon battered the two weakened spirits, binding the guardian and Ardie's ghost in tendrils of their corrupted essence. The two revenant Crusaders merged with their victims as they drained them to the dregs. All that remained on this plane was a transparent semblance as Jude wrapped his arms protectively around Ardie and rested his cheek on top of the other spirit's dark hair.

"It is over," the guardian said. "I hope I will be stronger next time."

"Skip the mushy stuff, just do it," Ardie said.

Jude cast his eyes heavenward and relinquished his flawed guardianship of the shining soul known on this turn of the wheel as Robert Andressen. The Creator called the guardian home, and the essence of Sean Red Dog was carried up as well. Unable to separate themselves, the revenants were pulled along like the tail of a comet. Rhys, James, and Gavin looked up as the air left the chamber in a sudden rush. For a moment, the men stood as though petrified, holding their breath, and then a fresh breeze ruffled their hair. The rogue zephyr smelled of salt water, with an elusive note of patchouli.

When the vagrant breeze soughed out, Rhys looked at his companions and raised an eyebrow. "Tell me you felt that too," he said.

Gavin nodded numbly. He had felt it and no mistake. There was no doubt in his mind that Sean Red Dog's spirit had just departed this plane. He didn't know how he was so sure, but he was, and that was that. He didn't explore the notion any further, just accepted it and moved on.

CHAPTER SIXTEEN

SIR ALUN'S triumphant sneer sagged when Richard and Odilon did not materialize right away. Again the revenant summoned the knights, but they did not answer. Casting the net of his arcane senses wider, Alun felt the last faint stirrings of the holy wind that had swept the chapel. With a roar of cheated rage, the Crusader's ghost turned his burning eyes on those arrayed against him. Swollen with the life force of his minion, he charged his foes.

Morgan leveled his spear and braced himself, as though facing a wild boar. Bo stood his ground in front of Tristan and looked for an opening as the Crusader rushed toward them. At the last moment, the knight swerved and engaged Bo. Pivoting on one heel, Alun put the bodyguard between himself and the Celt. Morgan swore as he maneuvered for a strike at the towering warrior in full armor. Tristan moved nimbly backward, staying behind his defender as Alun wielded his broadsword in a relentless attack. Bo caught the big sword in the crux of his crossed blades and sought to pull it from the knight's gauntleted hands. While the Crusader's weapon was blocked, Tristan darted out from cover to stab at the knight. Alun ripped his sword free and swung it in a great arc.

Tristan froze, swallowing hard as the point of the broadsword pricked his throat. Sir Alun smiled and opened his mouth to tell the others to drop their weapons, but he never uttered the words. The Crusader's breath left his lungs in a rush as Morgan's spear took him under the armpit. His arm paralyzed, the knight dropped the heavy blade with a ringing clatter. Bo sprang forward to finish their foe when a shimmering curtain of light enveloped Alun. The knight disappeared, and Morgan stumbled forward at the sudden lack of resistance. Bo stared at the empty space for a long moment before turning to Tristan. Gently, Bo touched the line of blood on the young man's neck.

"I'm fine," Tristan said. "Why did the revenant give up so easily?"

"Easily?" Bo said. "Were you watching? Morgan skewered the tin man pretty good."

Tristan shook his head. "No, that wouldn't do it. Did you see him? He practically radiated power. He'd fed, and recently."

"Why don't we return to… the real world?" Bo asked. "Or am I being extremely ignorant?"

Morgan looked at Tristan. "He doesn't know?" the Irishman asked.

"Bo," Tristan said, taking the man's hand, "we're on the other side here. Do you understand what I mean by that?"

"We're dead?"

"Not dead, but… dormant, I guess, is the best word. Our spirits— or souls, if you like—are in the unseen realm."

"Where exactly is this unseen realm?" Bo asked, sure he knew what Tristan was going to say next.

"It's everywhere," Tristan said. "It's around us and in us. It's the place in between places."

"Like the Force?" Bo said.

"Just like the Force," Tristan affirmed.

"This is no time to be discussin' *Star Wars*, even if it is a grand film. We must free your spirits from the revenant's control."

Tristan reached toward Morgan with his free hand. "Thank you," the liaison said. "You have fulfilled your destiny. You can move on."

Morgan hefted his spear, stained with the knight's evanescing blood. "I could get used to this guardian job," he said.

Tristan smiled. "There's only one place to apply," he said. "Take my hand, Morgan."

Morgan put his hand in Tristan's. "Morgan Idris in Heaven," he mused. "I hope the place doesn't self-destruct when I walk through the gates."

Tristan's smile broadened. "You're not so bad as you like to believe. Before you go... do you have any lingering regrets or grudges?"

"I was angry with the vicar for doin' me in," Morgan said. "But that turned out all right. I guess the bastard didn't see what a hand he was dealin' me when he killed me."

"Be at peace then," Tristan said softly.

Morgan grinned and raised his spear in salute as he faded to a shimmer on the air and winked out. Glory took him, and the backlash washed through Tristan and into Bo through the link of their joined hands. For several long moments, Bo stood blinking like a man who has lived in a cave all his life standing in sunlight for the first time.

"Um, don't we need him?" Bo interrupted hesitantly, shaking his hands to rid his fingers of the mild pins-and-needles tingle that moved through his entire body in a wave.

"He can't help us anymore," Tristan said. "And I'm beginning to think that we don't need anything but each other."

"You just made some connection, didn't you?" Bo said. "I see it in your eyes."

"There must be a reason the tides of fate keep washing us up on the same shore."

"Like bottles with messages in them?"

"That's a very nice analogy," Tristan said. "Tell me honestly… do you feel anything for me, beyond lust, I mean?"

"How do I know that what I feel is real and not what the… ghost wants me to feel?"

Tristan's eyes widened. "Shit!" he said succinctly. "You're right. Can you remember when we first met? Before we went into the castle together?"

Bo closed his eyes. He saw the young man climb with coltish grace from the boat and…. "Goddamn! When I first saw you, there were a few minutes when it was all so familiar that it didn't even strike me as odd that I was expecting you. *You*. Not some psychic I'd never met. I was waiting for you."

Bo's eyes opened and met Tristan's. "And then it was gone. Ardie was introducing you, and then you slipped and I caught you, and…." Bo words trailed off.

"Show me," Tristan said.

"Show you what?"

"What you saw when you first touched me."

"How? I don't even remember."

"Just don't be afraid," Tristan said bringing their foreheads together.

THE hunter reached the stony brow of the mound and approached the crude ring of sarsen stone cromlechs. He had never seen such a structure before, and stared curiously at the paired menhirs with their massive capstones forming an airy temple around a central altar. The stranger in a strange land walked through the phantom portal of one of the square arches and continued walking boldly toward those gathered within the circle. Though he was not prone to seek out other humans, he was intrigued by the mystery.

The man in the kilt of spotted fur who stood before the altar stone looked nothing like the folk who watched him so intently. Where they were short and stooped and shaggy, he was upright with slender, graceful limbs devoid of hair. He lacked the prominent brow ridge and heavy jaw; indeed, his features were as fine as a woman's of the hunter's clan. As the traveler watched, the strange one raised a bone knife and made a cut on his smooth, brown forearm. Bone ornaments rattled as red rain fell on the thirsty stone of the altar and sparked the crude miracle the newly converted faithful had gathered to witness.

The small crowd of naked near-humans roared a welcome as the Mother's avatar appeared on the sacred slab of stone that had fallen from the heavens. Dark of hair and eye and lithe of limb like the priest, with a sweet beauty that pierced the heart as well as the eye, the Goddess's representative on earth opened graceful arms in a gesture of greeting and benediction. A sigh rippled through the crowd as they felt the warmth of the Goddess's benison stir their loins. The sun-haired hunter made his way to the front, and the tribe fell silent. The priest waved the hunter closer, but the wanderer had eyes for none but the avatar, who beckoned to him in clear invitation.

"Come, man," the priest said in the hunter's language. "Come and take your pleasure. Scatter your seed upon this fertile offering."

The hunter frowned, golden brows drawing down over bright blue eyes. "I am a stranger. Why would you include me in your rites?"

"You have traveled far to be part of this ceremony," the priest said. "Do not be troubled, I traveled even farther. We are all in service to She Who Brings Life."

"Nay," the wanderer replied with bitter honesty. "I was cast out of my tribe as unworthy. I came here by chance."

The dark-eyed priest laughed, the small stones braided into his hair clicking together. "And I was cast out of my home when it was engulfed by the sea. I came here by chance, and these people have taken me into their hearts, despite my differences. In return, I share my knowledge, which they call magic."

The stranger's frown deepened at this speech. "I want no part of your ceremonies," he said.

"Ah, but you do," the priest said, showing a mouthful of perfect teeth. "For if you consent to lay with the avatar, you will be given a place of honor here. You will be a king and want for nothing. You will live out your days in such luxury as these people can provide."

"Why me?" the hunter asked as the crowd began to murmur at the delay.

The priest's eyes closed briefly as though he were unutterably weary. "I could tell you that your coming was foretold, and it would be true, for I foretold it. I could tell you that it is your destiny, and that would also be true, as I am a true prophet." The strange shaman leaned close, his obsidian eyes, outlined heavily in charcoal, glittering with deep emotion. "The plain fact is that we need your essence to quicken the avatar. These primitives are not suitable, but you are much more evolved, and marginally compatible."

The hunter blinked at the unfamiliar words. "You are mad," was his judgment.

"Please," the avatar said, in the sweetest voice the wanderer had ever heard. A soft hand lit on the hunter's forearm, and he turned to look into dark, liquid eyes. "Please?" the young man asked again.

The stranger frankly assessed the slender body with a half-smile on his face. "You are very desirable," he said. "But I shall get no children on you. You are a man, like me."

"Not exactly like you," the priest said. "Though Tris looks like a young man, he is more. He has the power to reach into the spirit world and speak with those who have passed over. If this tribe sees him as a god, I will not disenchant them. And if the worship of the Goddess survives, our exile here will not be a complete tragedy."

"Please," the young man repeated.

It was not until then that the traveler realized the young man was speaking another language. And though it was a language he did not know, he understood.

"The avatar has the gift of tongues," the priest said. "Come, man, do not be afraid. It is not so much that we are asking."

"What is my part in this?"

"The avatar has never coupled, for to do so would quicken the dormant seeds of his power. This was an event greatly feared by the high priest of my—" the shaman paused. "This can have no meaning for you, but I think my superiors were wrong. I believe that an empowered avatar would do Her will, not use the power to subjugate others."

"You are right. Your words have little meaning for me, but you do not feel like a liar."

"Help us. You can provide Tris with a source of compatible life energy." The priest smiled at the hunter's expression. "Do not fear. This energy is born of pleasure each time you bring satisfaction to the avatar."

"Your luck god must be smiling today. I was cast out of my tribe because of my love of my own sex."

"You believe it is luck?" The priest raised an eyebrow. "I have much to teach you, if you wish to learn. My land is drowned, but Her knowledge need not perish. Though you cannot beget children with the avatar to carry on our race, you can protect him and make sure that the worship of the Mother spreads and brings Her blessings to all men."

"Tell the boy you've found your stud," the wanderer said.

Tristan pulled back from the melding of his mind with Bo's. "So that's how it started," he said.

CHAPTER SEVENTEEN

BO STARED at Tristan in stunned disbelief. "Did that really happen?" he inquired incredulously. "Because it sure felt real."

"Those were your oldest genetic memories of the two of us," Tristan said. "We don't just die, you know. We go on, or at least that which animates us and makes us unique does. God, I sound just like Garry." Quickly, Tristan pushed his concern for Garry aside. He had no time now, if he hoped to salvage anything from the debacle he'd made of this situation. If he was ever going to prove he was a capable adult, this was the moment.

"But people don't keep meeting up down through history. Do they?" Bo asked.

"Don't," Tristan said, squeezing the man's hand. "Don't doubt… don't regret… don't despair. Those are the revenant's weapons. He doesn't want you strong, because he knows that you can defeat him."

"We, you mean," Bo said. "We can defeat him."

"I will certainly be a part of the equation," Tristan said lightly. "But you are the answer to this problem."

"How's that?"

"You really don't see it? You and Sir Alun are opposite sides of the same coin. If you turned to the dark, you would be him. If he fought for the light, he would be you."

"Why do I get the feeling there's more at stake here than I can appreciate just now?"

"Because you're a very perceptive man. Are you ready?"

"For what?"

"To go back, of course."

"We can do that?"

"I'm not saying it will be easy." Tristan smiled. "We come from the great well of the unseen realm when we're born, and our essences return to it when our bodies expire. In the waking world, the physical shells we left behind are animated now by the revenant's will. Our soul, our consciousness, is what we are here." Tristan paused.

"I get it," Bo said. "Our bodies are back there walking and talking?"

"Not at the moment, but they are breathing and performing instinctive functions."

"That's freaky," Bo said.

"Yeah," Tristan agreed. "Gives me the willies whenever I see it."

For some reason, the liaison's admission of fear made Bo feel better. "Zombies," he whispered spookily, making a bug-eyed face.

Tristan looked stupefied for a half-second and then smiled widely. "Flesh-eating zombies from Mars," he countered.

Bo shook his head. "For somebody who's an expert on the supernatural, you don't know much about zombies. They only eat brains."

Tristan nodded sagely. "So I guess you'd better watch your arse," he said.

Bo looked at the young man for a long moment, trying to decide if Tristan was making a joke or not. Tristan gazed blandly back, but a sparkle in his dark eyes gave him away.

"So that's how it's gonna be," Bo said. "Then allow me to retort that you might want to put on a cup, since you do all of *your* thinking with your little head."

Tristan snickered, his nose crinkling and his dimples dancing, and Bo's heart told him in no uncertain terms that this young man owned it now. *No, please,* Bo thought, *not again, not another drop-dead gorgeous young thing with the sexual agenda of an alley cat in heat and an appetite for my suffering.* Not after Troy and Jared and Chris... he couldn't do it again. He had vowed to Ardie that he'd break the pattern, and he would.

"It's broken," Tristan said. "I'm who you've been seeking in all those failed relationships. You're a hunter, Bo, a seeker, but your search is over. Be now what you were always meant to be."

Bo lifted his eyebrows.

"Do what you most want to do," Tristan said softly. "Do what your heart tells you."

"This reminds me of our first meeting," Bo said, as he took Tristan in his arms.

"It always does," Tristan murmured as the man's lips covered his.

"Do you hear me?" James shouted again.

"I don't think he heard you," Rhys said unhelpfully.

James steeled himself and pressed the point of the ancient dagger against Tristan's throat, playing his desperate hunch. "You listen to me, you evil bastard. You let my friends go, or I'll take away your power supply."

Gavin lifted an eyebrow, but refrained from comment as Tristan ceased rocking against Bo and turned his head toward James. Awareness seeped back into the psychic's eyes as they focused on the linguist. Then his gaze dropped to Bo's head, busy in his lap.

"Get him off me," Tristan cried out.

Gavin didn't hesitate. Grasping Bo by the shoulders, Gavin pulled the man away from Tristan. Bo did not react well to the interruption.

"Shite!" Gavin exclaimed as he tried to subdue the salvager. "Give us a hand."

Rhys stood like a deer in the headlights for a moment before he waded in and grabbed one of Bo's arms. "Fuck!" Lord Turcotte grunted. "He's a strong son of a bitch!"

"Can you reach my cuffs at the back of my belt?" Gavin asked. "I'm afraid to let go of him."

Rhys nodded and did as the policeman asked. Andressen fought like a berserker until the handcuffs were fastened around his wrists. As soon as the locks clicked shut, Bo fell unconscious.

"Oh God, he's not dead, is he?" James gasped as he moved forward. "Tell me I didn't kill Bo with that stupid mumbo jumbo from that cursed Big Ass Book."

"He's just passed out," Tristan answered as he finished straightening his clothing. "He's not as used to dealing with spirits as I am."

James sighed with relief. "That's the last time I dabble in black magic," he said. "Do you think I got rid of the ghost?"

"I think you gave him something to worry about," the liaison said as his glance skipped over the bodies on the floor. "I feel like I might pass out as well."

"Come and sit down in the main hall," Gavin said. "James, can you and Rhys manage Bo? I don't want to leave him here."

Rhys and James lifted Bo between them and carried him to the treasure hunters' indoor camp. Depositing the unconscious man on a cot, the other four gathered a short distance away. Tristan's gaze was drawn to the dagger hanging, forgotten, from James's hand. He touched his throat, and his fingers came away painted with red.

"Sorry," James said, offering a paper towel.

"You did what you had to," Tristan said, turning his gaze to Gavin. "So, are you ready to admit that there are more things in the world than you can prove with science?"

"I'm at a loss," Gavin said. "I don't know what to believe, or what to do next."

"There's nothing to be done until the storm's over," Rhys said. "And at least people have stopped dying for the moment."

"I hope Bo's okay," James said, looking guiltily at his boss and friend.

Gavin looked toward the chapel, his gaze intent. "Quiet for a minute," he said. "Hear that?"

Rhys nodded and walked toward the sound. In the generator-powered electric light, he saw something dark moving low to the ground near the chapel arch. Peering at the creeping shadow, Lord Turcotte made out a hand reaching up in supplication.

"It's Garry," Rhys said. "He's alive." As he knelt beside Garry, Rhys realized he had no idea what to do. The nobleman looked up in appeal and met Gavin's eyes.

"Easy, Dr. Arvel," Gavin said as he knelt. "That's a nasty gash you've got in your skull. Don't try to move or speak, please, until I can have a look at it."

Garry's coal-black eyes burned with the need to communicate as they fastened on Gavin's gaze. Garry's blue lips moved, but no coherent words came out. Gavin frowned and delicately parted the wounded man's thick hair.

"It's too matted with blood," Gavin said. "I need water."

James set the dagger down on the table and grabbed two jugs of distilled water from underneath another table. Popping the cap off one, the linguist offered it.

"Pour it slowly over the wound," Gavin instructed.

With steady hands, James directed the stream of water onto the gash and Gavin's hands. Everyone was intent on watching the policeman clean the wound as Garry continued to struggle to speak. Garry's eyes fixed on something over James's shoulder and grew wide with horror.

"Hold him, please, Sir Rhys," Gavin said as Garry moved restlessly.

"I think you might call me Rhys, considering present circumstances," Lord Turcotte said as he tightened his grip on Garry.

Tristan sank to his knees next to James. "Poor Garry," he said. "He looks as though he has suffered some brain damage."

"Quite possibly," Gavin said as Tristan reached out to touch Garry's shoulder.

Garry tried to pull away, and Gavin looked up at Rhys in mild irritation.

"Sorry," Rhys said meekly as he held Garry still.

"Shhh," Tristan soothed. "Do not fight so, Garry."

The parapsychologist's gaze locked onto his protégé's, trying desperately to communicate. The jagged bolts of pain that sawed into his brain had become one all-pervasive seizure of agony that was grinding away at his consciousness. The blackness yawned, and he was tipping into it, but something waited at the foot of the shadow gate. Something that hungered, something that would swallow his soul before it could cross over.

"Easy," Gavin said. "We're trying to help you, Dr. Arvel. No one wants to hurt you."

Garry shook his head, and Gavin cursed as he lost his grip on the man.

"Maybe there are too many strangers around him," Rhys said. "Perhaps Tristan can calm him, and then you can do your exam."

Gavin considered. "Makes sense," he said as he rose.

Rhys started to get to his feet, but Garry held onto him. Lord Turcotte bent down as Garry's lips moved frantically. Tristan stroked Garry's hand, pulling it from Rhys's forearm.

"Poor devil," Gavin said. "Wonder what he wants to tell us."

"All he said was 'not Tristan'," Rhys reported. "The benighted bugger is more worried about the lad than his own life."

Gavin nodded and then cursed again. "I don't believe it," he said.

Rhys turned and was surprised to see Bo Andressen, hands cuffed behind his back, moving along the floor like an inchworm. His vacant eyes were fixed on Tristan as he made his way determinedly forward.

"Single-minded fellow," Rhys commented.

Tristan turned his head and saw Bo. "Gavin," the young man called. "Keep him away from me, please."

Gavin stepped into Bo's path and gestured to Rhys to give him a hand. Both men grabbed one of Bo's elbows and hauled him up from the floor. They carried the writhing treasure hunter back to his cot and deposited him on it none too gently.

"Are we going to have to restrain him?" James asked.

"I'll sit with him," Lord Turcotte volunteered unexpectedly. "I'll call one of you if he gets to be too much for me."

"Thanks," Gavin said in relief.

"Gavin, Sir Rhys," the linguist called. "Did you move the dagger?"

Before either could answer, Tristan cried out for help.

Gavin, Rhys, and James hurried over to where Tristan sat with Garry's head in his lap. Garry's eyes were fixed, and his chest was still. Gavin felt for a pulse in the man's wrist and neck, and bowed his head in failure.

"I'm afraid he's gone," the policeman said.

Tristan looked up from his mentor's pale face. "What happened?" the young man asked. "He was trying so hard to tell me something, and then he just stopped breathing."

"I'm sorry," Gavin said. "Let Rhys and James take care of Dr. Arvel, all right?"

Tristan held tightly to Garry's jacket for a long moment and then let go. "I guess there's nothing I can do for him now," the liaison said. Gavin held out a hand and pulled Tristan to his feet. The psychic swayed slightly, and Gavin steadied him with an arm around his back. Tristan leaned against the big man's strength and Gavin wrapped him in a comforting embrace.

Gavin had comforted Tristan before, during the hours when a traumatized twelve-year-old refused to let go of his rescuer until Dr. Davies arrived. The constable had cuddled and soothed the lanky young man with the face of a Renaissance angel and found he was thinking how pleasant it would be to father a child. Small chance of that if his sexual orientation was known. He would have had to jump through every hoop in existence to adopt, and he hadn't the temperament to interview surrogate mothers willing to be impregnated with a homosexual's sperm. It was just another Joker that the hand of Fate had dealt him. Gavin surfaced from his gloomy thoughts and heard the odd noise that had brought him out of his depressing reverie. Why on earth had he dredged up those old disappointments?

"Tristan?" Gavin said, taking the strange noise for a suppressed sob. "It's all right if you want to cry."

Tristan raised his head from Gavin's shoulder and looked up at the man. For a moment, Gavin felt as though the floor was falling from under his feet at a rapid rate and his stomach fluttered queasily. He focused on the young man's dark gaze as a hand cupped his crotch. Gavin became hyper-aware that he was not holding a child as Tristan deftly handled his soft cock through his trousers.

"Steady on," Gavin said, taking hold of the liaison's wrist.

"I need you, Gavin," Tristan pleaded. "I need you to help me forget."

"Stop it, Tris. This is not the time or place for this."

"Kiss me once," Tristan begged, massaging the policeman's stirring shaft. "If you still don't want to fuck me, I'm sure I can find someone who will."

Gavin recoiled as Rhys and James came back into the hall. "You're not yourself," the policeman said. "Why don't you go and have a lie-down while I talk to Lord Turcotte?"

Tristan's sweet mouth curled in a barely concealed sneer. "Thank you for nothing," he said as he walked away.

The corners of Gavin's eyes tightened, but he gave no other sign of how much the words hurt him as he turned toward the other two men.

"Would you like me to go back and sit with Mr. Andressen?" Rhys asked.

Gavin glanced over at the bunkhouse area, where Tristan was just sitting down on a cot near Bo's. "He seems quiet just now," Gavin said. "And Tristan can call us if anything changes."

"Are you all right?" James asked Gavin. "You look exhausted."

"I imagine we all do," Rhys commented.

"Gavin didn't have those circles under his eyes before," James said. "He looks drained."

"Drained?" Rhys repeated as Gavin's head whipped toward him in sudden apprehension.

Gavin spun around and Rhys and James followed suit. All three men froze at the bizarre tableau across the hall. Tristan knelt beside Bo's cot. He had unbuttoned the blond man's shirt and bared the golden-furred chest. In his hands, Tristan held the ancient dagger, poised to plunge into Bo's heart.

Chapter Eighteen

"Bo," THE young man whispered against his lover's lips as the man crushed him in a fierce embrace. "You know what we need to do?"

"I want to," Bo replied.

Tristan smiled. "I've always thought it was a good thing that our salvation is linked to doing this. We seem to be reasonably proficient at it, and we don't mind the work."

"So, we love each other because we keep meeting down through the ages?"

"You've got it backward," Tristan said. "We keep meeting because of our love. We unite two branches of early mankind that gave birth to modern man."

"So psychic powers are...."

"Recessive Atlantean genes surfacing," Tristan finished for him. The young man paused before continuing. "I want you to know that I'm not a slut," he said. "Not that it should matter, but I was... I had never made love with anyone until the day I arrived at Caer Gwarchod and the revenant possessed me."

Bo lifted the young man's chin on his fingers and looked into the velvet eyes. "I admit that, in my mind, I called you slut and worse, but I can see that we were both manipulated."

Tristan took a deep breath and let it out slowly. "Okay," he said. "Everything's okay, then. Come on, Bo. Let's generate the power we need to kick this bedsheet's arse."

"Bedsheet?"

"That's what Garry called ghosts," Tristan said. "I used to think it disrespectful."

"It's time for some disrespect," Bo said. "What do we do?"

"What you do best," Tristan smiled. "Since Alun didn't kill us this time, we can complete the quickening ritual. We'll rub against each other until we spark the fires of creation. And then...." The young man's words trailed off.

"And then?" Bo prompted, nuzzling Tristan's ear.

"I don't know. It's never gotten this far before, I don't think."

Bo met the young man's gaze resolutely. "Let's not think," he said. "Let's take your advice and just be what we were meant to be."

Tristan raised his eyebrows and Bo grinned at him.

"Two people who can't stay away from each other," Bo clarified.

"Amen," Tristan said, just before Bo took his breath away with a passionate kiss.

Tristan responded eagerly, reciprocating every caress, pressing as close as possible to the man who set him ablaze with a touch. Bo possessed his lover with lips, teeth, and fingers as the young man clung to his strength like a flowering vine on a granite cliff. Without breaking the kiss, Bo lifted Tristan to sit on the altar. Tristan opened his legs and wrapped them around Bo's hips. Bo leaned forward, grinding his groin demandingly against the young man's, grasping the firm buttocks, kneading them as he made thrusting motions.

"You don't need to warm me up," Tristan gasped. "I'm ready for you."

"What about some lube at least?"

"This isn't real life, Bo," Tristan reminded.

"Oh. Okay then."

Bo ripped the cloth from Tristan's body, leaving the young man's sculpted physique draped in tatters. Pushing his trousers to his knees, Bo took hold of his aching arousal. In the purest rush of lust he'd ever felt, Bo seated his manhood and slid easily into the wet velvet. Tristan pressed his heels into Bo's lower back, urging the man on. Bo thrust again and buried his length in the pulsing tightness.

Welcoming heat envelops his spear as the barbarian sinks into the avatar's sheath.

A warrior-slave of the Mameluke Empire steals a moment of bliss with the Caliph's cherished dancing-boy.

A lovesick Elizabethan playwright writes a sonnet for his dark-eyed leading "lady" and is sweetly rewarded.

A Danish archeologist dallies with an Egyptian laborer while seeking a Pharaoh's tomb.

A soldier finds comfort in the arms of the Navajo codetalker he guards.

A twenty-first century treasure seeker stakes his claim on a young man who speaks to spirits at the same moment as a Pleistocene hunter merges with the last living link to a lost way of life. Their lips meet and meld as surely as their hearts and souls. They move as one in a ritual that transcends its physical origins, connecting the ephemeral to the eternal. Together they reach the peak of sensual stimulation, and critical mass is achieved. Ecstasy explodes in every cell in a barrage of bliss, a dancing white light that blows through them like a tornado of silver static charged with erotic electricity. Mere flesh could never withstand the inundation of power engendered by their union, but in this realm, it is absorbed until it leaks from every pore in a pearly glow.

"You look like an angel should look," Bo thinks just before overload takes him.

BO BLACKED out, and when he opened his eyes, he was severely disoriented. He felt as though he'd gained four hundred pounds, and his arms hurt. He focused on Tristan, who was leaning over him. It struck him then that he was back in the waking world, as the psychic called it. He was lying on his back with his hands bound behind him. Suspended above him was an ornate dagger, clutched tightly in Tristan's trembling fingers.

"What's going on?" Bo said as lightly as he could.

"Bo!" James shouted as Gavin and Rhys ran over.

"Stay where you are," Bo called back.

"Tristan's trying to kill you."

"Yeah, I can see that," Bo said. "He's… possessed, and the only reason he hasn't killed me yet is because he's giving the bastard the fight of his life. I'm going to try and help him, and I'd appreciate it if you guys don't do anything, no matter what you see."

James held up a hand to Rhys and Gavin. "Give Bo a chance," the linguist said. "I've seen him pull off one or two miracles since I've worked for him."

Bo rose slowly, until the point of the blade was almost touching his skin. Gingerly meeting the liaison's eyes, Bo searched there for the soul of his mate. "Alun," Bo said in challenge. "For millennia you and others like you have tried to destroy the last vestiges of the Mother's worship. You've come close many times, but you've never been able to stamp it out completely. Your faith is intolerant and inflexible. Anything different is an abomination. Any argument is heresy. Those that do not conform to your beliefs are damned. You aren't a torchbearer any longer. You've become the enemy of the light."

Gently, Bo kissed Tristan's wrist and the tip of the dagger drooped. "Tristan," Bo called. "I know you're in there, and I know you're strong, but if you need my help, tell me what to do, and I'll do it."

"He is not strong enough," Tristan said, an odd timbre in his light voice. "I thank you for the energy, though. Forgive me if I use it to destroy you."

"Tristan won't let you hurt me," Bo said confidently. "He's stronger than you think."

Tristan's merry laugh pealed out, but it had a manic sound. "He is already defeated. Did you really think a mere boy could stand against me? Look into my eyes and know the truth."

Bo swallowed as the dark eyes captured his gaze and held it. The revenant was not lying. Bo could see no trace of the gentle psychic in that hostile stare.

"Bo."

Bo held himself in complete stillness, hoping he hadn't imagined the small voice in his mind, and praying it came again.

"Bo. I love you," Tristan said. "Never forget that."

"Wait! What does that mean?" Bo shouted. Bo felt a soft breeze on his face, like a ghostly kiss redolent of cinnamon and musk and the faint briny scent of the sea. "No," Bo said, his heart pounding in suspicion.

"He is gone," the revenant said. "And this fine young body is mine."

Bo quickly pulled his knees up and brought his cuffed hands around to the front. Alun yanked Tristan's hands back as Bo reached out. Bo grabbed at the dagger, opening a cut along the edge of one palm as the revenant pulled it free. Bo snatched at it again, heedless of the damage to his hands. Alun moved Tristan's possessed body backward and put the blade to Tristan's throat.

"Don't," Bo said reflexively.

"I like this body," Alun said. "But I will bleed it dry if you take another step."

"Easy," Bo said. "I'm not movin'. Everybody stay back."

"Mortals," the revenant sneered. "So enamored of these husks of flesh."

"I'm particularly fond of that one," Bo agreed. "And you know what? You don't get to use it anymore. Go ahead. Use that fancy steak knife. I fuckin' dare ya!"

"Bo!" Gavin said, coming forward with the key to the cuffs. "Have you lost your mind?"

"Just started using it," Bo said. "If the ghost trashes Tristan's body, where will he go?"

"I can easily oust one of you," Alun claimed.

"Then why didn't you do that to start with, instead of going after Tris?"

On the last word, the treasure hunter launched himself at his enemy, tackling the slender body. The sharp edge of the dagger scored a line across Tristan's collarbones before Bo immobilized his wrist. Alun fought back, and the two men traded blows until the ceremonial knife flew out of the slim fingers and skittered over the stone floor. Tristan's body twisted in an impossibly supple move to grasp at the flying steel, but it skipped away from him. He crawled after it and Bo tackled him, stopping the revenant's forward progress by pinning him beneath superior weight.

"Get the goddamned knife!" Bo yelled.

James was already on it. Gavin changed course and knelt beside the struggling men on the floor. Rhys stood rooted to the spot, his head lifted in a listening posture. Bo and Gavin dragged the thrashing revenant incarnate to his feet as James approached with the dagger. The ghost fought harder as the linguist drew nearer, and the two men could barely keep a grip on the willowy body. James raised the poignard, and Alun grew still.

"Kill me," the revenant said. "And lose any hope of getting the witch back."

"I don't believe you," James said. "You'd say anything to extend your miserable life."

"You dare call me a liar? I am the lord of this place."

"No, you're not," Sir Rhys said over James's shoulder. "I am."

Tristan's eyes narrowed as Sir Alun hesitated before speaking. "We shall see," he said at last. "If you think you can challenge me, throw down your gauntlet."

"All right then," Lord Turcotte said and recited the words James had found in the Book. "As rightful master of Caer Gwarchod, I call upon all who have been wronged within these walls to present themselves for justice, should they wish it."

"No!" the revenant thundered in Tristan's refined tones. "Stop. Do not speak the words."

"Even the spirits of those wronged do I call upon," Sir Rhys pronounced in his vibrant baritone. "Any who have grievance against the bloodline, stand forth and receive justice. I call you once."

"Stop!" the ghost bellowed. "I command you!"

"I call you twice," his lordship said.

"No. Do not finish, or I will tear your beating heart from your chest."

Rhys calmly met Tristan's blazing eyes. "I call you thrice."

A boiling mist appeared behind his lordship and sprouted pale tendrils that broke off from the numinous cloud. The fog became several distinct columns of vapor that coalesced into vaguely human forms. In a few seconds, they resolved into the translucent figures of handsome young men.

"Cillian!" Gavin gasped. "Billy."

"Gryf," James breathed.

"Where is Chris?" Sir Rhys said doubtfully.

"Fool. You cannot be of my bloodline," the revenant said. "That one chose his fate, as did my other minions."

"As did you," Rhys retorted. "I feel not one scrap of sympathy for you, either. You deserve your fate. Let the wronged come forward and claim justice."

Slowly, the wan spirits of the young men the revenant had drained lifted their pale heads. The Crusader's ghost had absorbed their energy and naught remained but the signature wave on the ether that was their unique code. In this state, they were powerless, but welded together by a liaison, they were a formidable presence. Sir Alun's fear overtook his fury as he was smothered in an eldritch cloud of spent souls. These blighted spirits, denied their rightful rest, cleaved to the one who had snuffed them out like fireflies in a jar. Desperate to escape the cold, clinging ghosts who were drawn irresistibly to his spurious life energy, the revenant left Tristan's body and rose up to the ceiling. Gavin and Bo supported the liaison's limp frame as they stared in stunned fascination at the wisps of vapor that rose from his body, twining about the form of the long-dead Crusader. Sir Alun fought, tearing the mist to rags, only to watch it reform to curl about his limbs. His shrieks were silenced when the diaphanous shroud covered his face, sealing him in with his victims.

"Fuck me," Lord Turcotte breathed as the revenant disappeared in the roiling cocoon.

In a few moments, the last tatters of fog had dissipated. Nothing remained of the revenant, except for the havoc he had wrought among the mortals within the walls of the castle. Outside, the wind began to drop dramatically, as though the ghost's defeat were a signal. The survivors looked around at one another in patent disbelief that it was over. Bo moved first, looking into Tristan's still face and feeling for a heartbeat.

"Shite!" Gavin said. "Let's lay him down on a cot."

Bo knelt, clasping the liaison's cold hand as Gavin checked for a pulse. The policeman looked up and met Rhys's eyes, his face grave. James stopped in his tracks, the bloodstained dagger forgotten in his hands. Bo took Tristan's limp body in his arms and kissed the pliant lips as Gavin stood. Tristan's eyes opened, and his fingers moved weakly in Bo's grip.

Bo laughed through his tears. "You scared the crap out of me," the treasure hunter said.

"You do care," the psychic answered.

"I thought you were dead," Bo said. "Don't ever do that to me again."

"I *was* dead, but now I'm back."

"What are you saying?" Rhys asked. "That you've been resurrected? What does that make you, then?"

"Someone very special," Bo answered.

"I should say so," the nobleman remarked. "Am I bearing witness to the Second Coming?"

"This has nothing to do with Christianity," Tristan said, his voice becoming stronger. "Though it has a little to do with Jesus, since he was like me, or vice versa. It's so strange how things get twisted around after a few centuries."

"Such as?" Rhys prompted.

"Come on," Bo broke in. "The kid just rose from the dead. Give him a break."

"Sorry," Lord Turcotte said humbly. "Maybe Tristan will explain it to me later?"

"Is it really over?" Gavin wanted to know.

Tristan nodded and lay back, safe in Bo's arms, Bo's cheek resting on top of his head. Gavin grinned in relief and hauled them both up into a fierce embrace. James hesitantly held out a hand to Rhys. Lord Turcotte moved into the offered hug, and Gavin pulled them both in. The five survivors huddled together in the warmth and comfort of simple human contact. There is a lot to be said in favor of such comfort, but the linking of their spirits through the physical connection to the reborn liaison added a dimension of such richness and intensity that they were transported briefly above the crude matter that housed them. A silent accord was reached, and this band of brothers knew their paths would lie side by side for a long time to come.

EPILOGUE

"GRAND opening," Sir Rhys pronounced in his rich tones. "Grand opening. Lovely words."

James came close to rolling his eyes. "I fully realize that you're attempting to bait me with puerile euphemisms, but somehow I can't be angry with you when you're filling me up in such an agreeable manner."

Rhys came close to smirking, and then replied with exaggerated modesty. "I did have a little help," he said, glancing at Gavin.

Gavin smiled equably and rose from his sated sprawl to smack Rhys's ass, hard.

"Oh God, yes!" Rhys groaned. "Your sense of timing is impeccable, as usual."

James moaned with pleasure as Rhys's thick shaft moved almost imperceptibly in his sheath, rocking to the rhythm of Gavin's swats to Lord Turcotte's bottom. The linguist's starkly handsome features were transfigured by bliss when Gavin leaned over to suck strongly at the head of his arousal. Rhys groaned his approval as James's interior muscles rippled along the length of his aching shaft. James slid his fingers into Gavin's mane as the man took him deeper, and Rhys increased the speed of his stroke. With his other hand, the linguist took hold of Gavin's revived erection and pumped it enthusiastically.

Gavin stopped the spanking and gently, but insistently, prodded Rhys's rosette. "A grand opening," Gavin purred in his thick North Country accent.

James snorted with unexpected laughter and then convulsed with pleasure as Gavin went down on him again. The blunt head of Rhys's arousal brushed against James's prostate, and the linguist erupted in Gavin's mouth. Gavin swallowed, shunting his finger deeper into Rhys's passage, searching out the sensitive spot.

"Shite!" Rhys shouted as Gavin rubbed in figure eights.

James whimpered as the big cock sank into him to the hilt and withdrew briefly only to plunge into him again. Gavin took hold of the young man's thigh and pulled his legs farther apart. Tenderly stroking the silky skin where James's limbs joined his torso, Gavin took the linguist's lips in an ardent kiss. James moaned into Gavin's mouth as Rhys's stroke stimulated his sweet spot with each forceful thrust. Once again, James's lovers were taking him to the limits of bliss and then pushing him over the edge. Helpless against the adoring onslaught, a willing vessel for this rough, human magic, James responded eagerly with an abandon never seen in him outside the bedroom.

"I'm going to cum again," Gavin murmured as he relinquished James's mouth.

"Me too," James said.

"Touch yourself," Rhys requested, and James complied with alacrity.

In a few strokes, James came again. Rhys pulled his twitching rod from the linguist's sheath and rubbed it against James's as he spurted. James pulled Gavin forward by his pulsing arousal as the big man gave a cry of release and covered James's hand with seed. A knock at the bedroom door froze all three men in a Mapplethorpian tableau.

"Lord Turcotte?" a feminine voice called out.

"What is it, Kate?" Rhys called out.

"Your guests are early."

All three men scrambled from the enormous bed, searching madly for clothing shed in the heat of the moment.

"We'll be right down," Rhys said. "You needn't wait."

"Why would I, sir? I'm not curious," Lord Turcotte's chief of security replied. "I've seen the surveillance tapes."

Gavin chuckled at his colleague's dry wit as he tossed Rhys's shirt at the nobleman. "Sharp lass," he said.

"Disrespect is what passes for cleverness now?" Rhys asked.

"Kate's honest," Gavin corrected as he opened the door and went through it first.

As well-guarded and provided with alarms as the castle now was, Gavin still took the time to look up and down the hall before beckoning to Lord Turcotte. Rhys strode briskly into the corridor, followed by James. Gavin looked critically at his charge and fixed the collar of Sir Rhys's creamy linen shirt.

"Will I do?" Rhys asked.

"Admirably," Gavin said warmly, his glance straying to James. "Are you going to wear that tie?" the bodyguard asked.

"No," James said. "I'm going to use it in an assassination attempt later and I wanted to keep it handy."

Gavin rolled his eyes. "I think I liked you better when you were a mousy bookworm."

"A mousy bookworm?" Rhys asked. "I'm trying to picture such a creature… half mouse, half worm. I feel vaguely ill."

"What the hell's taking so long?" called the man just reaching the top of the stairs.

"They're probably going at it like famished sailors," someone answered from lower down.

"Bo!" James shouted and sprinted down the hall. "Tristan!"

Rhys looked at Gavin. "He's completely forgotten us," Lord Turcotte said.

His lordship's personal bodyguard smiled fondly at the insecure nobleman. "You've still got me," Gavin said, leaning to kiss Sir Rhys on the lips.

"You were right, Tris," Bo called. "Looks like they just got out of bed."

"Bo!" James reached his former employer and enveloped him in a warm embrace.

Bo hugged James back, trying to express with the fierceness of the gesture all that he could never put into words. These men had survived a unique and horrifying experience together, and there were some things that never needed to be said aloud again. Things that were understood, like the bond of love and purpose that united the five.

"My God!" James exclaimed, holding Bo at arm's length. "How long has it been?"

"Not that long," Tristan said as he finally reached the top of the stairs. "It was hard enough getting the man to agree to any time off at all."

"So, Bo," James said. "When are we going to dig up Atlantis?"

"We're not in the salvage business anymore, pard," Bo said gently.

"The hell we aren't," Rhys disagreed. "What would you call this place?"

"He's got you there," Gavin said. "Rhys may be graceless and temperamental, but he's also right a shocking percentage of the time."

Tristan smiled radiantly. "I like that," he said. "I like the idea that we're in the recovery business. But instead of ancient artifacts, we're salvaging people."

"Well, we will be," Rhys said. "The school is ready. All we need are some Atlanteans."

"I spoke with Alicia just this morning about the candidates we selected," Tristan said. "You'll not have a shortage of students. I like what I've seen of your staff, by the way."

Gavin's sharp ears noticed the ragged edge to the young man's voice. "Why don't we all go into Sir Rhys's sitting room and use it for its intended purpose?"

"I should meet Kate downstairs," Rhys said with genuine regret in his voice. "I'd rather be here catching up, but there are still a lot of things to coordinate."

"I'll help," James said. "Bo and Tristan love Gavin best anyway."

Tristan saw the look Rhys directed at James, a glance that mingled gratitude with adoration. It seemed the troubled aristocrat was mending well in the care of his loving therapists. James was smarter than a whole college of professors, and if there was something Gavin couldn't fix, Tristan didn't know about it.

Rhys looked startled when Tristan caught him by the wrist and kissed him softly on the cheek. "What was that for?" he asked. "Not that I'm complaining."

"Because you're handsome," Tristan said.

Rhys raised his eyebrows. "Just for being handsome?"

"And you smell good," Tristan added.

"Come on," James said, taking Rhys's hand from Tristan's. "Stop fishing for compliments, your lordship. Kate is waiting."

"And I'd rather see the nursery than all the rest," Tristan said.

"That's not a problem," Gavin said.

"I thought of something else I want," Tristan said.

"What's that?" both men turned attentively.

"Two husbands," Tristan said, flashing his dimples.

"You're just an avatar, not an actual deity, you know," Bo told the young man. "You're not above the law yet."

"Says you," Tristan grinned. "Can we go now?"

Gavin escorted Bo and Tristan back downstairs and they passed into the welcoming ambience of the nursery. Though there was room for forty infants, only one crib was occupied. The liaison made straight for the bed and leaned over the sleeping child. Gently, he touched the small, vulnerable head, stirring the silky curls with his fingertips. The baby's aura was as unmistakable as sunrise, but Tristan was still in awe of the banked power residing in this tiny, fragile body.

"Shame about his mother," Gavin said sincerely. "She was so full of hope when she came here."

"I remember," Tristan said, silently mourning the thin girl unaware of what she had carried to term, but knowing nonetheless that her baby would be special. "It was nobody's fault, though I should have seen...."

"Hey, you just said it was nobody's fault," Bo interrupted. "So this little guy has a lot of Atlantean blood, huh?"

The psychic touched his lover's hand. "Genes," he corrected.

"Wonder who his father was," Gavin said, not for the first time.

Tristan looked up, meeting Gavin's eyes. "We don't know this child's biological father," the liaison said. "I'll find out when he's a bit older, but for now I like to think that we're all his fathers. And I hope with all my heart that he'll have the benefit of guidance from each of us as he grows up."

Gavin had to force his words past a sudden tightness in his throat. "Even his lordship?" the bodyguard asked facetiously.

Tristan raised an eyebrow.

"Sorry," Gavin said. "I felt like I was going to cry. Had to say something fast."

"Because the big, bad caveman can't cry," Tristan said sardonically. "My God, Gavin, you're gay, act like it!"

Bo laughed, and the baby woke, blinking up at the blurry forms looming over him. His small face crumpled and his mouth opened on a wail of displeasure. Tristan scooped the child up and put him to his shoulder, rubbing his back and making soothing noises. The crying stopped as though a switch had been thrown, and the infant goggled at Bo with a wide toothless grin that caught at the man's heart. "He seems to like us," Bo said.

"That's convenient, since we'll be his teachers and his family for the next twenty years or so," the liaison said.

"We're not starting right now, are we?" Bo teased.

"I already have," Tristan said softly, turning the child to look into his eyes. "He says his name is Jude, by the way."

Bo and Gavin exchanged a look, but in the last three years they'd become accustomed to that sort of remark from Tristan. They'd seen enough evidence of what the psychic called the unseen realm to take the young man at his word. If Tristan said the baby's name was Jude, then that's what they'd call him. With a fond glance at the liaison, Gavin told Bo he'd meet them in the dining hall and went to take up his duties.

"Guess we've got a lot of work ahead of us," Bo said, putting his arms around Tristan from behind.

Tristan smiled as the man nuzzled the back of his neck. "A lot behind us and a lot ahead of us," he agreed. "Some of it will be in vain, and most people won't understand what we're trying to do, but you know that already. As long as we're together, as long as our faith in one another is strong, we won't fail. We'll make a better world."

"I'm behind you all the way, kid," Bo said, nibbling at an earlobe. "You want to go have a look at our accommodations?"

"In a few minutes."

Right now, Tristan wanted nothing more than to hold this child in his arms and feel the strength of the spirit that animated him. The liaison vowed that he, with the help of the other fathers, would provide

Jude with everything he needed to grow up strong, healthy, and safe. And in the fullness of time, this small life would change the world.

Working from the Arvel Institute at the refurbished Welsh castle, Jude would use his knowledge and powers to free his fellow men from the shadow of death's dark pinions. People would still pass away, for no one was meant to live forever in one body, but they would no longer fear it. They would learn and believe that death was not an end, just as the old faiths preached. For all religions were but pale echoes of the truths discovered in Atlantis.

Jude would show them proof, and Jude's offspring would spread the message. In two generations, Tristan knew, the dread of dying would become nonexistent. Freed from the fear of the unknown, mankind would awaken from their long nightmare into a dream that not only promised another life, but also gave corroboration of it. Released from these shackles, human beings would devote themselves to the improvement of life for all.

Tristan kissed the top of Jude's head as he placed him back in his crib. Jude whimpered, and the liaison whispered in a tiny, perfect ear. "It's all right. We'll muddle through somehow until you're old enough to take charge."

Tristan took Bo's hand and led him back upstairs to share the glory to which all who love are heir.

CONNIE BAILEY is a Luddite who can't live without her computer. She's an acrophobic who loves to fly, a fault-finding pessimist who, nonetheless, is always surprised when something bad happens, and an antisocialite who loves her friends like family. She's held a number of jobs in many disparate arenas to put food on the table, but writing is the occupation that feeds her soul.

Connie lives with her ultralight designer husband at a small grass-strip airfield halfway between Disney World and Busch Gardens. Logic and reality have had little to do with her life, and she likes it that way.

Visit her Web site at http://www.conniebailey.com/ and her blog at http://baileymoyes.livejournal.com/.

This is an expanded novel-length reprint of the novella *Revenant* originally published in the *Desire Beyond Death* anthology by Dreamspinner Press.

Also by CONNIE BAILEY

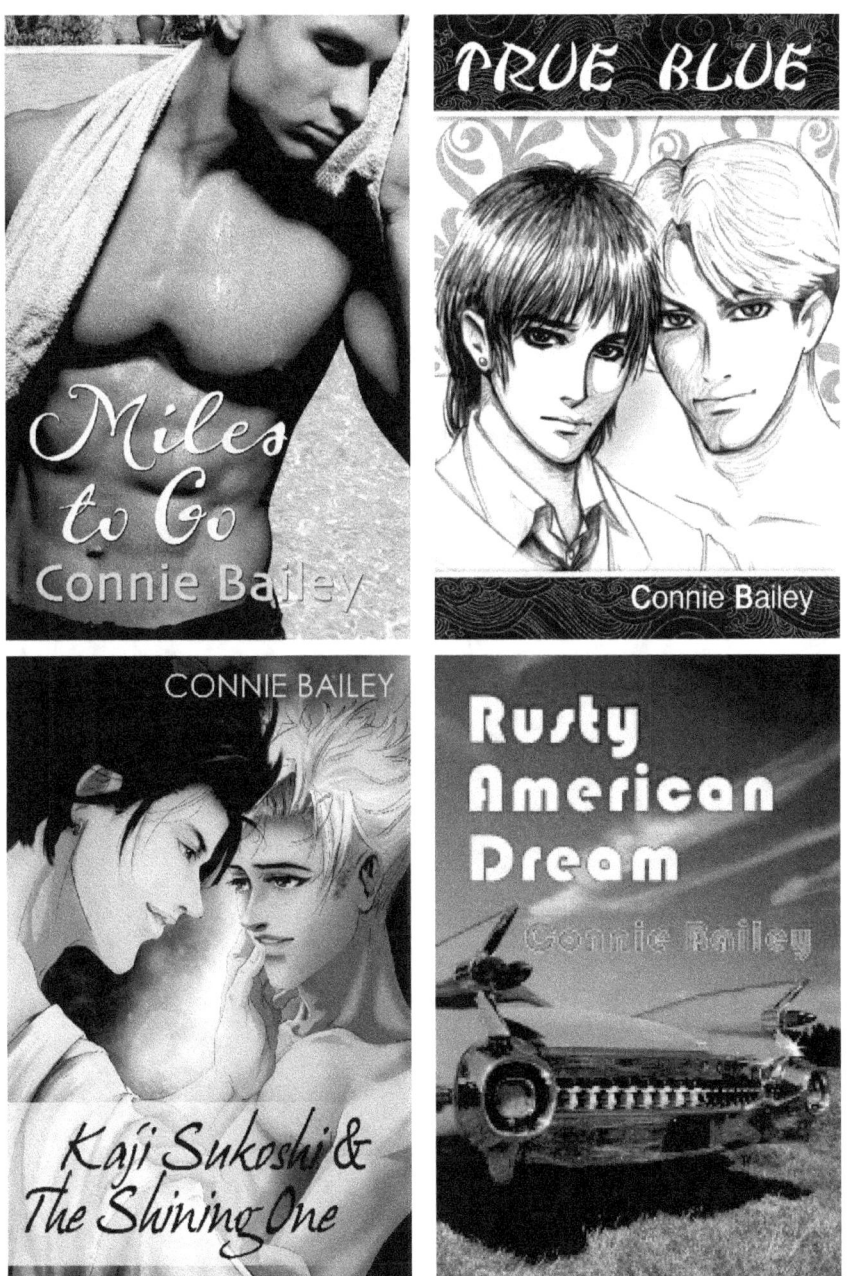

http://www.dreamspinnerpress.com

Also from DREAMSPINNER PRESS

http://www.dreamspinnerpress.com